JUST DRIVE

Just Drive
A speculative dark romantic comedy novella

JUST DRIVE

A speculative dark romantic comedy novella

Grace E. Kelley

Synthesis Press

TABLE OF CONTENTS

CONTENT WARNING

This is a novella intended for adults, as it does contain
explicit sexual content. (Chapter 10 if you want to skip.)
It also includes references to alcoholism, domestic violence,
emotional abuse, murder, death, and a loved one's battle
with cancer.

DEDICATION

For the ones who have spent their lives wondering—
Is who I am a gift? Or a curse?

And for Willy; you are my love through every roadtrip
adventure—even though you persist in taking unflattering
sleeping photos of me.

JUST DRIVE

CHAPTER ONE

Todd Does Something Crazy

TODD

THERE WERE WORSE THINGS than watching people die all day. The choked last breath, the way the blood pooled beneath their skin, the pallor that stole over their features, the unnatural stillness—Todd Mackewain was used to it all by now. At least, he told himself he ought to be.

The Gift had come to him from his grandmother when he was only eight; "Gift" being her words, not his of course. Todd didn't see how witnessing a mugging gone wrong the moment you locked eyes with someone—especially someone who had just passed by the entire line of empty urinals at the Yellow Hammer Travel Center, only to choose the one *right next to yours*—was anything other than grimly awkward. And how exactly were you supposed to make friends on the playground when the moment you met the eyes of potential-friend-number-one you saw his life tragically end in a crosswalk years later? The future was not written in stone, of

course, but the glimpses he gained from the first moment he locked eyes with someone revealed "the probabilities of possibilities", as his Gran had called them. Unless something or someone intervened dramatically in the current order of events, the future was already set in motion; the final domino just waiting to fall.

He'd been a friendly kid up until that point. But, for obvious reasons, at the age of eight he began preferring a lonely existence. He'd never told his mother why. He knew she'd never believe him.

"She has too little imagination," his Gran had said when he'd asked her why it was coming to him instead of to her own daughter. "She is so focused on certainties, she cannot see possibilities." She shook her head gently from side to side on her death bed, clicking her tongue like she always did when she knew she was obviously right.

But Todd wasn't quite sure what she'd meant.

Gran had insisted, up and down on her death bed, her papery hands tenderly stroking over the dark locks of his hair, that it was, in fact, a Gift and not a curse.

"You'll see someday, child. You'll see."

The memories flashed before his eyes as he stared into the foam of his pilsner and took his first swig. He sucked his teeth. It wasn't too bad—definitely drinkable. But it had that under fermented taste of a half-baked homemade beer. And he was pretty sure the owner of this tiny roadside bar in backwoods Alabama had no idea what a pilsner was.

Oh, well.

His mind turned again toward his last day with Gran. Because it had been her *last day.* Hers was the first death that flashed before his gray eyes just moments after she spoke those very words about The Gift she was passing along to him. In his eight-year-old's mind's eye, he'd seen her fragile ribs rise and fall just as the sun was setting outside her bedroom window. The sky was purple-orange. Her face

turned toward the light as she breathed in, as if sucking that beautiful fading light into the very core of her being.

She didn't breathe out.

The sound of a barstool scraping along the pine planks of the flooring drew his attention, and he glanced up to see the man who'd apparently survived into adulthood without understanding the bro code governing public restrooms.

"Huh...this seat taken?" the man asked after seeing the intensity of Todd's gaze.

"Nah, man. It's all yours," Todd said easily, and nodded to the empty stool. Considering the future, terribly violent end of the man's life, Todd found it in himself to overlook the man's lack of urinal etiquette. Besides, Todd had come out to the bar tonight for a drink and a little human companionship.

"I'm Todd," he said and extended his warm right hand, keeping his left on the pilsner impersonator.

"Steve." The man shook his hand, then removed his cowboy hat and settled on to the stool next to Todd, revealing a round head, his thinning hair trimmed uniformly short as if to disguise the loss. He was chewing a toothpick in the corner of his mouth, and removing this, he leaned his weight on his left hip in order to remove a hulking leather wallet from the back pocket of his Wranglers.

"Whiskey, neat," Steve said to the barman as he finally got himself arranged. The wad of bills in the wallet looked like hundreds from where Todd sat.

Was it disturbing to sit next to someone whose last moments you'd already witnessed?

Yeah, it was spooky as hell.

But, on the other hand, sitting next to Steve meant he didn't have to choose between avoiding eye contact with another stranger, or risk seeing another potentially gruesome death. For Todd, this was often the best that could be hoped for.

"What brings you out tonight Steve?" Todd asked, feeling friendly. He took another swig of his beer.

"I'm just passin' through," Steve drawled, "on my way to see my kid sister and her new baby in Castleberry. You?"

"I drive a big rig. Based out of Cincinnati. Just takin' a little roadside break before I pick up my next trailer and head north again."

"Aww, nice, nice," he said, pausing for barely half a second. "You make good money?" Todd choked on his beer.

"Enough," he said, inhaling through his nose. Perhaps the man's social ineptitude was not confined to urinal etiquette. "It's just me right now."

"Must be nice," Steve said oblivious once more. "No old lady back home holding you down." He gestured to the ring on his left hand with his stubby, right index finger and raised his brows meaningfully. He then took a too-long sip of the whiskey the barman set in front of him. Todd turned toward his pilsner again, which he suddenly found less repulsive to stare into than his present company.

People like Steve reminded him why he preferred to be alone. It wasn't only because he always hated that first look; the glance in their eyes which, no matter how beautiful, intelligent, or interesting, ended in the painful image of their death. Whether they were old and peaceful, or young and terribly tragic, or worst of all—violent at any age, it always ended the same.

No getting out of death or taxes.

He'd known that statement to be true his whole life. And The Gift never, ever let him forget just how little power anyone had over death in the end; just how weak and puny every single soul was in those final moments.

"Well, what do you do for a living Steve?" Todd asked, steering the conversation away from the painful awkwardness of his solitary existence, toward a safer, more interesting topic.

"What do you think?" Steve picked up his leather wallet and flipped through the bills, fanning them so Todd could see. As Todd had suspected, they were hundreds.

"Something in finance?" Todd smirked, the dimple in his chin shadowing further into the stubble. Steve reared back with a laugh that somehow reminded Todd of a braying donkey, and slapped Todd on the shoulder so hard he almost knocked him off his barstool.

"That's a good one Todd." Steve swiped at his eyes. "I guess you could say I'm in 'finance' in a way." He leaned in conspiratorially and a bit too close for Todd's liking. Todd could smell the whiskey and beans on the man's breath. "I'm a bookie."

"A bookie?"

"Yeah. A bookie… for the races." he stage whispered behind his hand, then took another sip of whiskey.

"What sorts of races?"

"Why the only kind worth paying attention to of course!" Steve leaned forward on his stool again and pulled a fresh toothpick out of the other back pocket of his jeans. He brandished it above his head like a magic wand before placing it in the corner of his mouth. He flicked the old one, split and chewed, onto the floor.

"The… Derby?"

"NO! NASCAR!" Steve slapped him on the back again. He was only halfway through one whiskey and he was acting drunk.

Lightweight.

Todd looked at his beer and realized if he were going to make an exit back to the quiet solitude of his truck cab anytime soon, then he'd better start drinking.

"Oh yes, of course," Todd said, taking a giant gulp. "Silly of me. Those racehorses are so last century." He was being facetious but Steve seemed as thick as they came. He took another long draft.

"I know, right? Glad to have someone around who finally thinks like me!" Steve proclaimed, and then, to Todd's horror, he raised his voice above the din of the small room and yelled, "Turn all the race horses into glue, that's what I'm saying! Who needs 'em?!"

And suddenly the eyes of every other person in the bar were on Todd and his clueless, tasteless , loaded companion.

There was a group of older gentlemen in flannel shirts and straw hats in a back booth who looked up in abject horror. They were followed by a group of younger gentlemen, their Carhartts and dirty T-shirts marking them as manual laborers. They were Todd's sort of people, he could tell, though he tried not to make eye contact with any of them. They knew not to take a man like Steve and his bluster seriously.

And then there was a group of ladies at a small round table by the front door. They were laughing. It was clear they hadn't heard a single word Steve had said and only looked up because of the volume of the disturbance. Well, that and the fact that their server, who was halfway through pouring the next round of drinks, seemed to also be looking. Her kohl-lined ice-blue eyes narrowed in judgement at Todd and his unfortunate companion.

And that was when he saw her.

Blonde hair cascaded over her bare shoulders in loose ringlets and she was wearing some sort of tiara. She was leaning her head back and laughing uproariously at something. She wore a simple knee-length white cotton dress adorned with a garish pink sash that said "BRIDE-TO-BE" in a curly script, and on her elegant feet, she wore comfortable-looking tan sandals. As she continued to laugh, she slapped her knee with her left hand which he noticed was adored with a too-large diamond ring. Todd realized the women accompanying her at that small table must be celebrating her impending nuptials by getting her rip-roaring

drunk—themselves along with her.

I hope she has a safe ride home.

With some reluctance, he turned away from the enchanting woman before her happiness could become his grief in the meeting of their eyes.

Then he turned his attention back to Steve, whom he realized, to his chagrin, had never. Stopped. Talking.

"So of course everyone assumes when you're a bookie on races it's about those dumb horses, and I'm like, 'no, man, why would I want to watch a bunch of animals run around in a circle with a bunch of skinny guys bouncing along their backs with their butts in the air?'"

"Mmmmm," Todd said, taking another large sip of his beer, raising his eyebrows and glancing furtively toward the door. He could make a break for it, but then he'd miss out on that delicious barbecue bacon cheeseburger he'd already asked the kitchen for. Maybe he could get them to throw it in a to-go container for him. Although this didn't really seem like a "to-go" container kind of place...

He decided to try for another subject change.

"So you're going to visit your sister huh? She just had a baby?"

"Yeah, man...three days ago. But, you know, her deadbeat husband has been using that kid as an excuse to not pay me the interest on what he owed me from last season and I've about had it." Steve slammed down his empty whiskey glass and ordered another. "So I figured, now that the kid's out, I'd come on up. Pay the happy family a little visit." Todd's jaw dropped.

Welp. Subject change didn't help. Like, at all.

Then, suddenly, out of his periphery, Todd saw a blonde head coming toward the bar on unsteady feet. She leaned between them and ordered another pitcher for her table, and Todd couldn't help but notice she smelled like summer strawberries.

"Sorry, y'all," she said drawling heavily in her inebriated state. Todd studiously avoided her gaze. "Sisters need another pitcher!" She tossed a twenty on the counter and began carrying the pitcher back to her table and the waiting group. Todd smelled something almost as delicious as the blonde woman's hair and began sighing in relief as he saw the barman carrying a mouthwatering burger toward him from the kitchen. His stomach growled.

Finally.

But his eager anticipation was short lived because, a moment later, he heard the scrape of a chair leg and the crashing splash of a full pitcher of beer, and knew the beautiful woman with the strawberry-sweet hair had just gone down.

Todd leapt off his bar stool, and the next thing he knew, he was leaning over the woman's stunned face. Her eyes were a deep cerulean blue. As her gaze slid to his own, he heard his Gran's voice in his head. She was reminding him, as she always did at the start of his visions, that "This is only the probability of possibilities…"

He saw the woman with the strawberry hair and cerulean blue eyes lying on the ground. She was in much this same position as she'd been the moment before, but now her blonde hair, fanned about her face, was turning red as blood pooled around her. There were hand-shaped bruises around her throat and she was wearing a white dress: A wedding dress, Todd realized. The pearls dangling from her ears were splashed with blood and her fingernails were ragged from clawing at the hands and arms of the man who now stood over her. Where there had been laughter, there was now only terror and shock in her eyes. Before the vision ended, Todd noticed that the man was wearing a shiny, new ring on the ring finger of his left hand.

Todd jerked back to the present, shaking his head.

"Whew!" she said. "That was quite a spill!" As if realizing her double entendre, she started laughing even harder.

"What's your name?" Todd asked, still looking into her eyes—some part of him relieved to see the lightness and joy returning from the frightening vision he'd seen in them just a moment before.

"Mar-ge-ry," she drawled, drawing out the syllables much longer than he imagined she'd be doing sober.

"Nice to meet you, Margery, I'm Todd. May I help you up?"

"Todd...that's a nice name, Todd," she said as he helped her to her feet, keeping his hands on her elbows until he was sure she was steady. "Cute chin dimple, too," she said, swaying toward him and tapping his chin once with her perfectly manicured finger.

Shit.

Todd felt like he'd just been struck by lightning.

"Margery! You spilled the pitcher!" the plump redhead at their table whined.

"Maybe you should get home," Todd said gently, backing away slightly.

"Yeah..." she said, looking longingly over her shoulder at the group of her friends. She seemed suddenly sober. Not actually sober, of course. But quiet...thoughtful. "I don't think the girls are ready to leave yet. But I am getting married tomorrow...Lord knows I need my beauty rest."

"Sure, sure. Wouldn't want any dark circles for the big day now, would we?" Todd said, swallowing hard. He was fighting to stay calm, but even as the words left his mouth, all he could think of were the dark circles of hand prints around her throat, and the dark circle of blood beneath her head.

Tomorrow. She dies at the hands of her new husband TOMOR-ROW.

Horror choked him as she smiled at him once more,

her hand trailing down the sleeve of his flannel shirt as if reluctant to let go of his steadiness. Then she stumbled back toward her friends, narrowly avoiding the giant puddle of beer with her unsteady gait.

"Todd?" Steve called out from behind him. "Are you even listening to me?"

It was in that moment Todd knew he was about to do something crazy. He called out to the barman.

"Can you put my burger in a doggy bag? I think I'll take it to go."

Thirty minutes later, Todd was driving out of the backwater town that was Brewton, Alabama, with an unconscious Margery riding shotgun in the cab of his truck.

After he'd left his subpar beer at the bar with a generous tip and told Steve to "stop carrying around so many hundreds for the love of God," he'd turned his charm and his chin dimple on the group of women who called themselves Margery's friends. His suspicions about the nature of their friendship were confirmed, in that it hadn't taken much convincing at all, to persuade them it would be "no trouble" for him to give her a ride home because it was "right on his way." He was an old childhood friend, after all. Didn't Margery remember seeing him at Jim Bob's graduation party last year?

She'd gone cheerfully and was passed out against the cab window before they even hit the interstate; a line of drool snaking its way down her chin.

Todd learned another sad lesson about humanity that night, and that lesson was this: If you are too drunk and too lazy to care about the bride you are supposed to be celebrating, to drive her home at a reasonable hour the night before her wedding, then your pretty friend might just be kidnapped by a strangely "gifted" truck driver who has decided to do the insane thing and try and save her from being murdered on her wedding night.

These things do happen from time to time.

CHAPTER TWO
Somewhere Outside Nashville

MARGERY

MARGERY WOKE WITH a roaring in her ears and the feeling that a hatchet was lodged between her eyes. She squinted blearily, and saw only the dim lights of the dashboard and the running lights down the aisle between her and the man who had offered to drive her home last night.

"UUUUUUUUUGGGGGHHHHH." She let out a groan to capture the ache in her head and the disorientation in her mind, as she tried to remember what, exactly, had happened last night.

"There's ibuprofen in the top drawer of the side table." The driver twisted his head slightly to project his deep voice, with the slightest hint of a southern twang, toward the back of the truck. "And there's bottled water in the mini fridge!"

Turning to her left side, she saw the table and the small fridge and made for them, but her legs were all tangled in

the charcoal sheets of the lower bunk of the big rig and she had to thrash a bit to get free.

"Why ME?! SUUUUUUUCK!" she let out, as she toppled the foot and a half out of the lower bunk to the floor of the cab. She kicked her legs maniacally to get free of the sheet, and after another few seconds of struggle, she finally righted herself.

"You okay back there?" the driver asked. She could almost hear the smirk in his voice so she ignored him, rummaging through the top drawer of the built-in bedside "table". She found the pills just where he said they'd be and plopped back down on the lower bunk. A sudden wave of nausea hit her, and she leaned forward, putting her forehead on her bent knees and breathing deeply.

In through the nose, out through the mouth.

"Water's in the fridge!" the ever-helpful voice of the driver called back again, and she figured he could hear she'd found the pills but hadn't opened the fridge yet.

A moment later the nausea passed, and she opened the door of the small fridge and popped the cap off the water bottle. She gulped greedily, then popped the pills and leaned back against the wall, letting her eyes drift closed again. If only this headache would go away, then maybe she could think straight.

"We'll be stopping for breakfast in about an hour, if you're hungry," the voice called back, "but there are a few granola bars in the second drawer if you need something to tide you over."

Her stomach growled as if in answer, and she began reaching for the second drawer, figuring putting something other than water and painkillers in her stomach would probably be a good idea. But as her fingers brushed the knob, Margery stiffened. At the sight of her perfectly manicured nails, something vitally important she was supposed to be doing at that very moment suddenly clicked into place.

Food first. Then I'll deal with this startling realization.

Yanking open the drawer, she snatched a granola bar and lurched to her feet. Slowly, she shuffled down the short aisle toward the solid shoulder of the man driving. He was wearing the same red plaid shirt he'd been wearing last night, and from his haggard expression, she guessed he'd been driving all night. She fiddled with the wrapper of the granola bar.

What was his name again?

"Todd?"

"Yes, gorgeous?"

"Where are we?"

She stared out of the windshield, noticing the horizon lightening in shades of pink and orange over the tops of the trees.

"About thirty miles outside of Nashville."

Her heart began hammering in her chest. She took a bite of the granola bar.

"Tennessee?"

"That's the place."

His voice was calm. Matter-of-fact. Reassuring. But she could not be reassured.

"But I can't be in Tennessee!" she sputtered around a mouthful of granola bar, then swallowed. "I'm supposed to be getting married at First Methodist in Brewton, Alabama at 4pm today!"

Shawn will be furious.

A fresh shot of fear raced its way down her spine.

"Not anymore, you aren't."

His fingers flexed on the steering wheel ever so slightly. Margery gripped the back of his seat as a slow fear uncurled itself in her already unsettled stomach. She took a step back.

"Take me back."

"I can't do that, doll."

"And why on earth not?"

"Because *you* asked me to drive."

"I what?"

"Last night, I was getting ready to drop you off at your parents' place, but you told me you were having second thoughts. Something about your groom-to-be scared you, you said. Something wasn't right. So, you told me to just drive."

"I did?"

"Mmmmhmmmmm," Todd said, not meeting her gaze as she continued to gawk at him in the rearview mirror. "I tried to convince you that coming with me was not the only way to get out of the union, but you were quite insistent. You tucked yourself right into that lower bunk and passed out."

"Oh," she said, her face flushing. At the same moment, she found herself flooded with a strange relief, but it was quickly swallowed by shame.

What kind of woman am I, that I'd skip out on Shawn the day before our wedding?

And then, another shot of fear.

Shawn will be furious...

She could see it in her mind's eye—the way she'd come home late one night from time out with the girls, only ten minutes later than when she'd told him she planned to be home. She could still feel his rage as he towered over her in the entry hall, hissing, "Where were you?" as he gripped her shoulder, fingers digging between her neck and collarbone. "Shawn...you're hurting me," she squeaked, trying to laugh off the uncomfortable moment. But he hadn't let go. And she'd never been able to forget the way his eyes blazed pitilessly, his very gaze threatening to turn her into ash on the breeze.

"I'm sorry if I put you out..." she said, shaking her head to clear the memory.

"Not at all, not at all," Todd assured her. "I've been needing some company. And, besides, I can quite honestly say I've never had a cab mate quite so lovely as you." His eyes swung to the dog collar hanging from a hook near the center of the windshield, the early summer light glinting from the metal tag where it swayed to the rhythm of the road. Margery looked down at herself and frowned. Her white dress from the night before was now rumpled, and her "BRIDE-TO-BE" sash was dangling from the armrest of the passenger seat. Her sandals, for some reason, were on the dashboard. She'd woken up enough mornings after the girls had gotten her wasted, to imagine what she probably looked like—smudged makeup, tired eyes, the curls smooshed flat on one side of her head—and cringed.

"You're only saying that because you have to keep your eyes on the road."

"You forget I drive for a living, doll. I can feel the road as much as I can see it."

The roguishly handsome face turned towards her, and his gray eyes scanned her from head to toe in a way she suspected was intended to be flirtatious, but it somehow carried in it the edge of concern. Then Todd smiled a crooked smile at her, his chin dimple deepening beneath the dark brown of his stubble, before dragging his eyes back to the road.

"I guess," she said, the ghost of a smile curving her lips upward. She swallowed at the heavy lump in her throat but it remained. The plastic of the disposable water bottle crackled as she opened it again and took a swig. "So..." she said, "breakfast?" The sun was just starting to peek above the horizon, and with it, the darkness and fear in her own heart seemed to lessen. Not only the short-lived fear she had been kidnapped, but something else—something about what Todd had said she'd mentioned last night—about her second thoughts. But she wasn't really afraid of Shawn...was she?

Or have I just been too afraid to admit my fear of my own fiancée?

He'd shoved her to the couch in the middle of the disordered living room, strewn with beer cans, a box of crackers, and spray cheese. The TV blared in the background as Shawn rounded on her once again. "Who is he? Who's the other man you're seeing?" She could feel herself trembling where she tried to sit up awkwardly amongst the cans on the couch. The beer on his breath stank as he leaned in, grabbing her by the back of the neck, and hissed in her ear, "I promise I'm not mad baby...I just need to know his name."

She shook her head to clear the thoughts. Of course there hadn't been anyone else. She'd just lost track of time... and he was drunk. Shawn loved her. She knew it. He was just...protective. Right?

Then why do I feel so relieved to be hundreds of miles away from him?

Todd continued.

"There's this great little mom-and-pop place on the edge of Nashville. They have the best hash browns you've ever had in your entire life and pancakes the size of your face." He turned toward her, emphasizing the word *face* by blaring his eyes and dragging his bottom lip emphatically through his teeth. Then he smiled slightly, nodded to the passenger seat meaningfully, and turned back to the road.

"Wow...sounds impressive," she said, raking a hand through the underside of her flattened hair and sliding into the seat beside him, her eyebrows raising slightly as she snatched her sandals from where they'd been discarded on the dashboard.

"You don't sound convinced," he said. She bent in half, working the straps of her shoes around her ankles.

"Well, just because the pancakes are the size of my face,

doesn't mean they taste any good." She managed to get one of her shoes buckled.

"Ohhh! I didn't know you were a pancake aficionado! Now I'm really glad I brought you with me."

That infernal chin dimple deepened as he grinned at her like a Cheshire Cat. She began working on the second shoe.

"I'm not, it's just, I know that size isn't the only thing that matters!" She finished the buckle and started to take another swig of her water, but then choked as she realized what she'd just said. Her cheeks flushed and she could feel her chest suddenly spreading with those embarrassing red splotches which had been the bane of her existence her entire life every time she was flustered.

"True," Todd agreed, his head dipping slightly. She could tell he was pretending he hadn't also heard the unintended innuendo, and was deeply grateful. That was until she heard the next words out of his mouth.

"Well I can assure you these pancakes are not only HUGE, but they are, in fact, *delicious*."

She stared out the window, squinting at the cars merging onto the freeway, trying not to look directly at the rising sun, which wasn't exactly helping her headache. As if noticing her squinting, Todd grabbed a second pair of sunglasses from the compartment between their seats and handed them to her.

"We're almost there," he said easily, grinning at her again. And she wondered what it must feel like to be so unruffled.

So free.

TODD

BETSY AND MIKE'S was exactly as Todd remembered-it. The large blue-and-white striped awning out front, the

chime of the diner door, and most importantly, the stout man standing behind the cashier's counter. He wore small metal frame reading glasses at the end of his nose, but still he was leaning away from the sheet of paper, his eyes widening like he'd seen something either very funny, or very shocking. He wore his usual, garish Hawaiian shirt; the peach hibiscus blooms weaving in between neon-green leaves. The shirt, if it could be called a shirt and not a catastrophe, was tucked into soft, stained blue jeans. Atop this, the man wore a large apron with "Betsy & Mike's" written on it in faded blue thread, the tail of which seemed to be coming loose. At their approach, the man pivoted towards them, keeping his eyes on what looked to be an invoice.

"Welcome to Betsy & Mike's, would you like a booth or a..." he stopped talking as he glanced up. His ruddy cheeks widened as his eyes lit up behind his readers. "Todd? Is that you son?"

"Sure is." Mike's eyes lingered on Todd's face even as he made his way around the counter and embraced him in what could only be defined as a grizzly bear hug. Todd felt the stress of the past twenty-four-hours retreat from him, ever so slightly, with every thumping pat from the large man's hand on his back.

"It's so good to see you again," Mike said, keeping his hands on Todd's shoulders and squeezing softly. "You've been gone from us for too long."

"I know..." Todd said, regret coloring his voice. "But to make up for it, this time I've brought a friend." Mike's warm blue eyes shifted to Margery where she stood at Todd's elbow, looking...well she still looked beautiful didn't she?

Even after she changed from her rumpled dress into an easy pair of gray sweats and a pink T-shirt with a bedazzled 'TENNESSEE' emblazoned across the chest—the best they could find in a pinch at the truck stop before coming across the highway for breakfast—Todd could hardly take his eyes

off her. She'd washed away the makeup from beneath her eyes, and after fussing her manicured fingers through her blonde hair, she'd swept it over her shoulder into a loose ponytail, the remains of last night's ringlets doing their best to shine in the stream of sunlight coming from the eastern window of the diner. Todd was still wearing his customary red plaid button-up over a black T-shirt and his favorite worn-in jeans. His leather boots scuffed softly on the checkered linoleum.

"And what a lovely friend she is," Mike said, his eyes wide as if trying to rein in his shock. "I'm Mike," he said, extending a hand as he released Todd and pivoted toward Margery.

"Margery," she said, her voice wavering uncertainly, but with a glance from Todd something in her seemed to straighten as she added, "I take it you are the man with the pancakes?"

Todd bit his lip to keep from laughing but Mike seemed to have no such compulsion. All at once, as if the spell of Todd suddenly walking through his diner door had broken, Mike let out a low rumble, that built to a chuckle, and ended with a sound that reminded Margery of every TV adaptation she'd ever seen of Saint Nick. Mike wiped at his eyes.

"Yes darlin', I do have the pancakes. Let's get you folks to a nice cozy booth and Betsy'll come and take your order."

Mike led them to a back corner booth with a view of the rising sun, carefully drawing the blinds down low enough so they wouldn't be blinded by the glare until the sun reached the top of the awning. Then he hustled over to the coffee pot behind the bar and yelled, "Heya, Betsy, Todd's here!" The booth was comfortably worn, but clean as always, and within moments, Todd and Margery were facing each other, a steaming cup of the best diner coffee in each of their hands.

"Great mug," Margery commented, turning the white porcelain back and forth in her hands and sliding her fingers in and out of the handle.

"The mug?"

"Yes. The mug. It's a great mug."

"I don't follow." Todd schooled his face into a look of befuddlement, but he couldn't stop the twinkle of mischief in his eyes.

"I thought you said you'd been here before."

"I have. Thousands of times."

"And you've never noticed the mugs?"

"The mugs?"

"The mugs!" He saw the flush rising in her neck and tried to hide his smirk. "Haven't you ever noticed how they fit perfectly in your hand? How the handle is large enough for all of your fingers to wrap through it? It's a good mug! It's a great mug! I'm not loony for thinking so."

"Oh yeah..." Todd said, looking down at his own mug and noticing the way his large hand felt holding it, like he could instantly relax.

Like I'm home.

"I guess I never noticed before." He could almost hear Margery rolling her eyes.

"Men!" she huffed beneath her breath.

"What was that?" Todd asked, having heard her perfectly well.

Just then, a gray-haired woman with a pixie cut appeared with the menus, her smile as bright as the sun. She wore a clean yellow blouse with tiny rosebuds on it, and, like Mike, a pair of soft, yet serviceable blue jeans. A gingham apron was tied snugly around her slim waist.

"Well, would you look what the cat dragged in!" she said, the smile widening the laugh lines of her angular face.

"It's good to see you, Betsy." Todd said, his lips tipping up in a roguish grin. "And, may I say you are looking especially radiant this morning." Betsy's eyes flared as she half-heartedly snapped Todd on the shoulder with the menus she still held in her hands.

"And you, Todd, are as shameless a flirt as ever." Betsy turned her eyes toward Margery. "And who is this lovely companion?" Margery's face began to flush even further, and she opened her mouth to speak, but Todd interjected before she could get the words out.

"This is Margery. She's...an old friend of mine."

"Really?" Betsy said, peering inquisitively at Todd over her tortoiseshell frames, the beaded chain swinging a bit with her exaggerated motion. "An old friend....of yours?" He could tell she was thinking of saying something else, but her lips pursed as though she'd immediately decided now was not the time or the place for this conversation. Instead she turned warm eyes on Margery and smiled again. "Welcome to Betsy & Mike's, Margery. We couldn't be more thrilled to have you." She looked between the young couple a moment longer, then said, "I'll give you a moment with the menus," before hustling away.

Todd opened his menu and began studying it like he didn't already know exactly what he was going to order. He could practically feel Margery boring a hole into his skull with her eyes.

"You were messing with me weren't you?"

"About what?"

"About the MUG!" she huffed. "You know perfectly well it's a good mug and you just had to pretend you didn't know what I was talking about to make me...I don't know!"

"Mad as a hornet?"

"Yes!"

Todd flashed her his most charming grin.

"I'm sorry Margery. For some reason I just couldn't resist the temptation. You're kinda cute when you're flustered, you know? Not at all like those nasty stinging creatures."

He flipped his menu up onto the table and continued to study it, dragging his pointer finger down the list of options as though it were the roadmap to his next destination. But

flashing his eyes over the top of it for the briefest of moments, he caught a glimpse of Margery's mouth opening and closing like a fish caught on a line.

Thirty seconds later, as if sensing he was about to get himself into serious trouble with the only girl she'd *ever* seen him with, Betsy appeared at their sides.

"Ready to order?" she asked, sharp eyes trained on Todd with a look of loving reproach.

"I'll have the pancakes," Todd said, "with a side of extra-crispy bacon and some hash browns, please."

"The same for me," said Margery, smiling sweetly at Betsy before turning a glare toward her companion. "I just can't wait to take a giant BITE."

CHAPTER THREE
Pancakes & Big Decisions

TODD

"JUST WHAT DO you think you're doing?" Betsy whispered urgently the moment Todd stepped out of the bathroom.

"Going to the bathroom..." Todd said with a raised brow, feigning his confusion.

"Todd Rollins Mackewain! You know very well what I mean. What are you doing, *with her*?"

Todd stared, his mouth opening and closing. He'd never been able to lie to Betsy— not since he was the ten-year-old neighbor child who spent more of his time in Betsy and Mike's kitchen than he did in his own.

But, of course, there was always a first time for everything.

"Don't you like her?" Todd asked, pretending to be affronted. "Because I know the bedazzled 'TENNESSEE' shirt might be a little much, but she cleans up real nice I promise." Betsy smacked his arm, and there was nothing playful

about it.

"You know very well, I wouldn't care two figs if she walked in here wearing a paper bag, Todd Mackewain. What *I do care about,* is that sparkly rock the size of a goose egg on her left hand. I know *you* didn't give it to her. *So, who did?*"

This stung a little, though Todd couldn't put a finger on exactly why. He'd chosen a lonely existence after all, only breaking his rule once—for Nelson. Todd pictured the slobbering bulldog mix who had been his faithful canine companion for over a decade, and a smile quirked the corner of his mouth.

When he'd stumbled upon a cardboard box labeled "free puppies" outside a bar one late fall evening in Missouri, he'd intended to walk right past. The box had looked empty anyway, and he hadn't had a dog since he was very young. But then he'd heard a heartbroken sound and decided to investigate. When he peered over the lip of the box, there was one wrinkly pup left, his wide eyes full of sorrow and longing and the night was turning cold. Though Todd's gift only worked on humans, he'd seen enough deaths to know when a fellow creature was in trouble. Before he even knew what he was doing, Todd had picked up the sorrowful pup and tucked him inside his flannel jacket. He'd skipped the bar that night and driven to a pet supply store instead—and Nelson, as though knowing just how lucky he truly was, let his stubby tail wag freely as he rode in the passenger seat that first long drive together.

Someone ought to know the truth. And it may as well be Betsy.

When he looked back toward her, her lips were pursed. She was studying him the same way she had when he was a boy stealing cookies from the ceramic cookie jar on the kitchen counter the moment she turned her back.

"Fine," he said, "I'll come clean."

Betsy waited, her caring face inscrutable, but her eyes light-

ened with the beginning of his confession. "We met at a bar last night, and I didn't mean to, but I looked into her eyes and saw...I saw her death and..." He looked down, fiddling with a loose thread dangling from the second-to-lowest button hole on his worn flannel shirt. He was trying to find the words to express the horror of what he'd seen, and the subsequent necessity of the insane choice he'd made in the aftermath.

"Todd," Betsy spoke gently, putting a soft hand on his arm, "you know I've known about the gift, even before it was your own, and I know the gift has often been a source of incredible heartbreak...but there's nothing you can do." She laid her weathered palm against his stubbled cheek and turned his face toward her. "You know that as well as I do."

"But what if there was?" It was almost a whisper.

"What?"

"What if there *was* something I could do?" He searched her face for a sign she might understand.

"Todd..." she began, her eyes misting with tears.

"Betsy, she dies TODAY. At the hands of her new husband."

Silence fell between them, and Betsy went very, very still. Her fingers went cold where they still sat on his cheek.

"How...how awful..." she managed to get out. Her lips parted in horror and her hand dropped back to her side causing Todd to shif uncomfortably.

"I need to get back," he said.

"Yes," Betsy agreed, "she'll be missing you." She turned slowly and walked back into the kitchen, as though hypnotized.

MARGERY

"Y̶OU WEREN'T LYING about these pancakes," Margery said around a mouthful as Todd slid back into the booth.

"MMMMMM! And this *syrup*. What do they put in this syrup?" She lifted up the glass syrup container and turned it in the light as though doing so would allow her to see the ingredients. Setting it down, she swallowed her bite of pancake, and gathering a stray bead of maple syrup with the pad of her finger, popped it into her mouth. She was feeling worlds better now that she had food in her belly. "MMMMMM!" she exclaimed again. Todd Chuckled.

"It's what they *don't* put in the syrup," he said. "Most greasy spoons like this one use that high-fructose corn syrup 'pancake syrup' crap. But not Betsy and Mike. They get theirs from a farmer friend up in Wisconsin. That right there is Grade A one hundred percent *real* maple syrup." Margery's eyebrows rose slowly at the declaration, suddenly feeling a little sheepish about how much she'd poured onto her plate of pancakes, assuming it was the cheap stuff.

"Good to the last drop," she said, swiping her finger along her plate again. Todd finally began to tuck into the pancakes that had arrived from the kitchen while he'd been in the bathroom. For some reason his eyes kept flicking back to Betsy in the kitchen, his face a mix of emotions Margery couldn't quite understand. She cleared her throat.

"They seem nice."

"Who?" he said, turning toward her so fast she thought she heard his neck crack. He winced ever so slightly.

"Your...*family*."

"Oh. Yeah..." he said, rubbing the sore spot with his left hand. "Betsy and Mike...they're great. They didn't raise me exactly, but they looked after me after my grandma died. My mom was working two jobs just to keep us afloat, and Betsy and Mike...I spent every day after school at their house." He glanced up at her, his eyes shining with a fragile sort of vulnerability. He took another bite of his pancake.

"My mom was gone a lot too," she said, sparing him from having to immediately explain. "After my dad left—

and *it was good he was gone,* if you know what I mean—but after he left, money was tight. Real tight. And my mom always wanted the best for me you know? She wanted me to take dance lessons like she never got to, and she wanted to move us to the nicer neighborhood on the west side of town...but the bills were a lot with one waitressing job. So she picked up an early morning shift delivering newspapers too."

"That must have been hard," Todd said at last, chewing thoughtfully, his chin dimple appearing and disappearing with each bite of pancake he consumed.

"I didn't mind it so much," she said, watching him, "except the part where I woke up alone."

"And what did she think?" he asked.

"Of what?"

"Of your fiancée?"

"Oh." She chased the few remaining blueberries around her plate with her fork. "She likes Shawn...I mean...liked him, okay, I guess. He didn't like me spending much time over there, but she was so busy anyway, and honestly...she just wanted someone to be there to take care of me in case..." Her fork stopped moving and her lip began trembling. *Don't cry. Don't cry. Don't cry.* "In case, she didn't make it."

"What do you mean?" Todd asked, his forehead lined with concern. His gray eyes trained on her face with all the force of a

metal detector divining coins in the sand.

"She..." Margery took a breath. "She had cancer," she said at last. "Pancreatic. Stage two, so they think they got it with this last round of chemo, but you know how these things go...it..." She paused again, her fork lodged in a blueberry, her eyes locking on his. "It really shook her up." Moving almost in slow motion, she popped the blueberry into her mouth.

"And you, too, I'm sure," Todd said, taking another bite, his gaze locked on her face as though he'd stared into the

maw of death a thousand times and lived to tell the tale.

"Yeah. Me, too."

"And does he?"

"Does who? What?"

"Shawn. Take care of you?"

Margery froze, her fork suspended above the second-to-last of her blueberries. The world went blurry as sudden and unwelcome tears filled her eyes.

Shit.

"He...he tries," she said, trying to collect herself by staring at her plate. Todd reached across the small booth and grabbed her left hand where it was balling up the paper napkin.

"Margery," he said, almost in a whisper, "I know I haven't known you very long, and I know I am, as Betsy would call me, an 'incorrigible flirt', but please hear me when I say this: Trying isn't good enough."

"I know, but he...."

"TRYING. ISN'T. GOOD. ENOUGH." Margery glanced up from her plate, and what she saw in his eyes shocked her. This was not the dispassionate care of a stranger, but some emotion lost between anger, sorrow, and desperate hope. He was watching her. Waiting. To see if she understood, maybe?

"I know," she found herself saying aloud. She lifted her napkin and wiped the corners of her mouth. And even though she didn't remember the conversation that led her to being in Tennessee with Todd this morning, she knew the woman she had been last night had made the right choice—*somehow.* She had to trust that decision. "I know," she said again more firmly this time. "Excuse me. I need to make some calls." She pushed up from the booth and pulled out her phone, scooting past another group of patrons to make for the door. As she did, it was like a weight had miraculously been lifted by three simple words—

"The wedding's off."

TODD

Todd FELT RELIEF wash over him, quickly followed by an unrelenting terror as he had two thoughts almost simultaneously;

1. *"Thank God she isn't marrying that murderous asshole."*
and
2. *"What am I going to do when she finds out that I lied to her?"*

MARGERY

THERE WAS A settledness in Margery she hadn't felt in years. After the long hug goodbye with Betsy and Mike, and promises to let the road lead them back again soon for more pancakes the size of their faces, Margery and Todd walked back across the highway towards the big rig.

"So..." she began, "what now?"

"What do you mean?"

"I mean...you've been so kind to me...a complete stranger. Apparently driving me out of town when I asked you to, even though I was SUPER drunk. Then feeding me the most delicious pancakes of my life...," She paused, tucking a stray piece of blonde hair behind her ear.

"Don't forget introducing you to the wonders of *real maple syrup*." Looking up, she saw he was watching her face intently as she spoke again.

"Yes, that too. You've been so kind. But…umm…I was supposed to be getting married today and now—" She stopped short.

"Now, what?" His gray eyes were soft and kind. They held none of the teasing from a moment before.

"Now…I don't exactly know what to do."
They reached the cab of Todd's truck and stopped for a moment. Todd turned to face her, looking thoughtful.

"Margery, the way I see it, you've got a few options." Margery stood, silently listening, her arms crossed over her bedazzled chest. "One: We can get in this truck and I can drop you off at the nearest airport with a flight back to Ala—"

"I don't want to go home," she said before he could finish. A flush of heat raced across her cheeks.

"Or…," Todd began smiling, "we can get in this truck and you can join me for an impromptu cross-country road trip. As long or as short as you'd like, I promise. I'm a contract carrier so my work takes me to more scenic locations than average." Margery knew the curiosity must be sparking in her eyes at this description, and she had no wish to hide it. Todd smiled. "I can offer you an excellent playlist, the best roadside snacks a trucker can offer, and though the "accommodations" are a little mean, I promise to teach you how to roll out of the lower bunk without falling on your face." He was smirking now, but Margery pretended to ignore it. She blushed again as she recalled the way she'd indelicately flung herself free of the sheets just that morning.

"Sounds like a good way to spend your time," she said after a moment. "Road tunes. Snacks. Seeing beautiful places. Meeting interesting people…"

"You, Margery, are the only interesting person I have met in a long, long time." His eyes flicked back to hers and she stared at him for a moment, unsure of what to say in response.

"So you're saying you don't take it upon yourself to rescue every drunk damsel in distress that needs a ride home, then?"

"Well..." he said with a flirtatious gleam in his eye, as if he'd always say yes to rescuing drunk damsels. "well...no." He sighed and ran a hand through his hair, almost seeming embarrassed. Then, grinning again, he said, "I try not to pick up anyone who isn't wearing either a tiara, or some sort of bedazzled T-shirt, at least."

"Good," Margery said, turning toward the cab once again. "I'd be embarrassed to be seen with a trucker who picked up just *any old cargo* off the side of the road..." Todd opened the passenger side of the cab and she attempted to clamber in gracefully, but failed, her foot slipping on the very first step. Todd put a hand out to stop her fall and it landed on the side of her hip. Her face flushed. *I'm going to need some better shoes if I have to do this all the time.*

"Careful, there," Todd said, "I don't want my passenger princesses to fall and break her royal neck before we've even gone anywhere interesting." He'd removed his hand as soon as she was steady again, but Margery could feel her chest going splotchy regardless. She found herself reluctantly grateful for the godawful T-shirt she was wearing.

"I'm no *princess*, believe me," Margery sniffed, trying to regain some dignity and composure as she climbed into her seat. She leaned over and yanked the cab door shut right in Todd's infuriatingly dimple-chinned face. As she stared out through the windshield, trying to cool her cheeks, she saw the day was mostly overcast, but the sun still managed to poke its head through the breaks in the clouds every so often. It was a perfect day for a drive. A moment later, Todd swung himself behind the wheel.

"Well, Margery," he said, clicking his seatbelt and prompting her to do the same, "as long as you're riding in my truck, I plan on treating you like a queen, especially

while you're wearing that shirt covered in *jewels*…" Margery rolled her eyes.

"Just drive, Todd."

"It would be my pleasure. Which way shall we go? North, or south? Here in Nashville, there is a variety of loads I could pick up that will take us to all different destinations, and I'm the dispatcher's favorite so I leave it to you, my *Passenger Princess*."

"Let me guess, you flirt shamelessly with the dispatcher in order to get your own way." Todd smiled and winked as she gave him a sidelong glance.

"I find a little friendliness smooths the road to everyone's satisfaction." He paused again, studying her face. "So, Margery, what'll it be? North, or south?" His eyes still gleamed with mischief as he glanced at her, but something about his air seemed to respect the gravity of the moment— of the choice. *Her choice.*

Margery had never felt so free.

"North," she said.

CHAPTER FOUR
The Road North

MARGERY

"W HERE DID YOU say we were going?"

"I didn't say," Todd smirked at Margery from his place behind the wheel. "But it's somewhere...sweet." Margery scrunched her nose.

"We've been on I-65 for hours, and hours, Todd and..."

"Correction," Todd broke in, "we've been on I-65 for one and a half hours."

"Well, it feeeeeeels like forever, Todd!" Margery huffed, slumping back in her chair. "And I'm hungry." Todd just laughed and tossed her a bag of trail mix from the console between their seats.

"Those pancakes didn't last long, did they?" He smirked and gave her another sidelong glance she barely caught out of the corner of her eye.

Margery's lips turned down into a frown, but she grabbed the bag greedily and pried the zipper top open with her manicured fingers, then stopped, surprise coursing through her.

"Is this homemade trail mix?"

"Yes…" Todd raised his brows and tipped his face towards hers.

"But you're…a trucker…", she stammered, unable to put into words the reason for her surprise.

"Yes…" Todd said again in the exact same tone as before.

"And you have to stop for gas like fifty times a day!" She could feel she was blushing but she didn't care. She was on the onramp to what felt like a very big discovery about this man she'd only recently met, and she had questions that needed answers.

"Actually, the tank on this thing is gigantic. I only have to fill up, like, every sixteen hours or so," he said.

"But you have to stop all the time anyway to pee, right?" Her voice was getting higher pitched by the second.

"I'm not a robot." Todd seemed caught between laughter and some sort of unknown insult. Finally, the question made sense enough in her head, it came flying out of her mouth. "And when you stop to pee, you don't just…buy your snacks at the gas station?"

Todd laughed again, big and loud.

"What? What's so funny?" The peach color in her cheeks was turning a deeper red every moment.

"I'm not a walking stereotype, Margery. I'm a person… who happens to like his homemade trail mix better than that expensive, and might I say, disgusting, store bought crap. Half the time the nuts are rancid in those things."

"I did read an article about that once, I think," she said. "My friend, Trinity, has this crunchy mom magazine I end up reading whenever she's doing my hair at the salon. But, Todd, it doesn't make sense! Here you are, driving across the country for days at a time, and you don't even like road snacks?"

"Oh I love road snacks. Just not those kinds."

"And except for trail mix that you apparently make for

yourself in your..."she swiveled her head towards the back of the cab.

"I do it when I'm home every few weeks. Buy stuff in bulk and mix it all up in my apartment kitchen, then pack it up for the road."

"Okay...and your apartment is where exactly?"

"Cincinnati."

"Obviously. Okay, so you mix up your trail mix, and you take it on the road and..."

"And granola."

"What?" Surprise was going to be a familiar feeling when traveling with this man, she could tell.

"I make my own granola too."
Margery was silent for a moment before she said, "Are you a secret hippie,Todd?" He laughed again, and something unfurled in Margery's chest at the sound of it, as a surprise turned to an unexpected delight. Todd wiped his eyes.

"With the exception of the gas guzzler I drive in order to facilitate the transport of goods around the country...I guess you could say that."

"You hug trees, don't you?" Todd flashed her a wicked grin she felt all the way down to her toes.

"Only in Wisconsin," he said.

"Is that where we're going? So you can go and hug your friends the trees?"

"You'll just have to wait and find out," Todd smirked, and Margery rolled her eyes at him, but the thrill of adventure was a song in her blood. *He's not what I expected...is he?*

She'd known danger before, but somehow, she'd never felt free. Not like she did with this near stranger who managed to put her at ease, no matter how much he seemed to simultaneously unsettle her.

"But first, we'll make a stop at one of my favorite little spots for lunch. I'm looking forward to introducing you to the kind of 'road snacks' that I like to enjoy."

"If they are anywhere as good as this trail mix," Margery said, around a mouthful of pretzels and dark chocolate chips, "I can't wait."

Almost two hours later, Todd and Margery stopped at a greasy-looking food truck with "Bubba's Fried Chicken" stenciled in spray paint on the side. Margery raised her brows in question at the sight of the place, but Todd only smiled and ordered a heaping basket of drumsticks and bone-in thighs for them to share. When they got back to the truck after a necessary pitstop, the combination of the crispy fried chicken with the homemade slaw and pickles made Margery groan. It was good—too sinfully good.

"How do you always know where to find the best food?" she demanded.

Todd only smirked and said, "I'm always on the hunt for the magic no one else seems to see."

They didn't linger long. Todd said they needed to keep a brisk pace if they were going to make it to Chicago by dinner time, though he hadn't said where they'd be going after that. The man liked to keep his secrets; of that much Margery was sure. But as they drove, and ate, and drove some more, Margery found herself telling Todd a few of her own. What she'd always wanted to be when she grew up, for one.

"I wanted to be a fairy princess of course," she said, making Todd laugh.

"Sure, sure. But when you were slightly older than three? What about when you knew what some of your real options were? What did you want to be then?"

"Honestly...I'm not sure," Margery said thoughtfully. "I knew what I didn't want to be. I didn't want to be stuck in a loveless marriage with a loser husband...and I didn't want to worry about where the next paycheck was going to come from."

"Sometimes knowing what you don't want is the first step." Todd agreed.

"I mean my Mom loved me. So much. But she wasn't really there. She was so busy working to give me the life she thought I wanted, she wasn't able to really live life with me."

"That must have been hard," Todd said, turning his face toward her. She blushed as his eyes drifted over her face.

"No harder than what you went through, I'm sure," Margery said, turning away, uncomfortable.

"My challenges don't lessen your own suffering," Todd said, sounding so certain Margery couldn't help looking over at him again. His eyes were trained on the road, but there was a tick in his jaw that raised the hairs on the back of her neck. He took a deep breath and the moment passed as he returned to his previous line of inquiry. "But surely you wanted to be something besides a fairy princess—though that is certainly a noble pursuit." Margery laughed for a moment, and felt relief and surprise in her chest.

"You're right, of course," she said, her eyebrows pinching together. "I wanted to be an artist. Watercolor painting was my favorite. I took a class in high school—absolute best three hours of each week. Every time I had a brush in my hand..." She paused then added, "the voices in my head just got quiet, you know? It was just me and the watercolor paper. Just me and the brush. I could make something be just the way I wanted it to be—I could paint the world in my own colors...and make beauty out of..." She trailed off, gesturing with her hand, trying to find the words.

"Out of nothing," Todd said suddenly, his eyes still on the road. "You made beauty out of nothing."
She nodded grateful that he understood and went on.

"But, you know, no one ever makes money off their art, so it kinda would have prevented me from succeeding at a lot of those 'don't want to' goals I had." She brushed the remaining fried chicken crumbs off her lap with the back of her hand and grabbed another napkin from the glove compartment. Already the cab of Todd's truck was starting

to feel like home.

"If only fulfilling the dream was as easy as having one," Todd said at last, changing lanes to go around a slow-moving tractor.

"If only," Margery said, looking out the window again. For awhile, the cabin again lapsed into companionable silence until Margery picked up the thread and spoke again.

"And what about you?"

"Hmmmm?" Todd asked, as if startled out of some dark train of thought.

"What did you want to be when you grew up?"

"Oh, I don't know...probably a garbage man?" Margery laughed.

"It's true, I think all little boys want to be a garbage man at some point. I have these little cousins, Bobby and Benji—they're about five and three—and they think there's nothing better in the world than the idea than the idea of holding on to the back of a garbage truck."

"It's a very important job," Todd mused, nodding seriously.

"It is!" Margery agreed. "Their mom, my Aunt Celia, is always so good about elevating the importance of every job. She never laughs at them for wanting to be garbage men and when I..." She trailed off.

"When you...what?" Todd glanced at her again, and she felt like he was seeing right through her.

"When I have kids someday...*if* I have kids someday, I hope I can be the same. None of that classist crap only elevating white collar jobs. Our country runs on the work of so many uncelebrated, blue-collar workers, yet they are so often devalued and treated as less-than. That doesn't seem fair now, does it?" Margery blushed, a sign of her agitation and passion, and slyly slid her eyes in Todd's direction to see how he'd respond to her statement.

"As one of the 'uncelebrated' people you mentioned..."

Todd smiled, "I agree with you, completely."

"You were an essential worker during the pandemic, weren't you?" Margery asked before she could think better of bringing up such a painful time in recent history.

"Yeah. Pretty damn essential. Hardly any of us could get any time off to even get home for a few days during that time...not with the dramatic increase in shipping demands nearly overnight."

"That must have been so hard for you. Weren't you lonely?"

"Nah, not much more than usual. I had my buddy Nelson, with me then." His eyes shifted to the dog collar hanging from the hook near the middle of the windshield. Margery followed his gaze and paused. The sudden grief rolling off of her new friend was palpable, and she thought she saw silver lining his eyes before he blinked and it was gone.

"How long ago did he pass?"

"About a year ago," Todd said.

"I'm so sorry Todd," she said. "You must miss him."

"I do..."Todd said, "but I'm not too disappointed in my new cab mate. She's pretty, and she's kind, and she doesn't drool nearly as much as a bulldog mix." Margery smacked his arm playfully.

"I don't drool AT ALL, Todd." She rolled her eyes.

"Oh, yeah?" He said, sliding his phone free from its place on the center console. "Then what do you call that?" Todd handed her the phone, which he'd opened to the photos, and there was a picture of her from earlier that morning, her head tipped back in sleep, mouth wide open, and to her abject horror—there it was—a tiny line of drool snaking its way down toward the mole on her chin.

"TODD!!!" she screeched, alarms blaring in her head. "YOU DID NOT TAKE THIS GROSS PICTURE OF ME SLEEPING!"

"It's not gross," Todd said, snatching the phone from her

fingers before she could delete it. "I think it's kinda cute."

"CUTE! CUTE?! Why I just...I JUST..." She could feel her face had gone as red as an early spring radish, meanwhile, Todd looked perfectly composed, a small smirk playing about his full lips. And that damned chin dimple. Margery couldn't get another word out, but her mouth kept working like a catfish on a line, while her body tried to digest her embarrassment and rage.

"Speechless, I see. My charm does have that effect on women from time to time," Todd said, stroking the stubble on his infernal chin.

"You know what?! Charm, schmarm—you are a creep, Todd Mackewain! A creep who takes gross pictures of help-less passengers while they are lulled to complacency in the cab of your truck after gigantic pancakes!"

"If you say so, Margery," Todd said, smiling.
It wasn't until they'd been sitting in silence for another hour or so, Margery quietly recalibrating her inner calm, and Todd seeming to drive smugly, if that were possible—that Margery realized he'd never actually answered her question about what he'd wanted to be when he grew up.

TODD

HE WAS PLAYING a dangerous game and he knew it. Margery was everything he'd never imagined he could have: smart, beautiful, kind and funny, and yet, Todd knew he couldn't let her get close. He'd already revealed too much. Taking her to see Betsy and Mike had definitely been a mis-take, and now she was asking him insightful and adorable questions about things like what he'd wanted to be when he grew up.

Okay, he knew he'd started that line of inquiry. Still he hadn't expected her to turn it back on him so quickly. Maybe

he was surprised because most people he talked to didn't really see him as someone worth getting to know. He was just a trucker—just some guy driving around America in an endless loop making sure everyone got their deliveries on time—and no one had ever really cared to get to know him on a personal level. But Margery was different. She saw him in a way Todd wasn't sure he'd ever been seen before. He could almost sense her tiptoeing around the secrets she knew he was keeping, even as she tried to know him more.

And now he was fucking terrified.

He tried to let the rhythm of the road lull him into a sense of peace, the way he had always done after he'd seen a particularly grizzly death in the eyes of a stranger. The way he always did after he hung up the phone from his once-a-month call with his mom. But all he could do right then, was to plaster that nonchalant smirk on his face and just keep his eyes facing forward.

What the hell am I doing?

He'd practically kidnapped this woman. Technically, he had kidnapped her, initially, even though she chose to continue with him after that first night. It was still a bit of a grey area as he knew she was journeying with him under semi-false pretenses. She thought that she, herself, had decided to make a break for it, but Todd had decided that all on his own, and on her behalf. And even though he'd had no doubts at all the night before that it was the right thing to do, the light of a new day and Betsy's voice rang in his ears.

"There's nothing you can do."

There were different schools of thought on this of course. Betsy and Mike, who had known about the gift when it had been his grandmother's, tended toward a more conservative understanding that fate was fate, and there was nothing you could do to change it. Most of Todd's life he'd lived by this rule. But the moment he'd seen Margery's death in his eyes, he'd heard his grandmother's words again—*the*

probability of possibilities—and he couldn't shake that maybe, just maybe, there was another way.

He didn't want to keep living like a shadow of death. What if, instead, his gift could bring someone life; someone like Margery? *What if my gift could save a life instead of only predict when that life would be taken?*

A couple of hours later, despite the fact he'd shown her the photo he'd snapped of her sleeping that morning, Margery was fast asleep again. This time, her chin tucked toward her chest, and Todd could see the faint movement of her eyes beneath her lids. He could only imagine what was going on behind those eyelids. What was she dreaming about? The wedding she was supposed to have been going through right at that very moment? The thought made Todd's hands tighten on the wheel until his knuckles whitened.

But when a stray hair from Margery's loose topknot fell forward as her head dipped even further in sleep, a wave of deep tenderness threatened to sweep him away. He reached over and gently tucked the strand back behind her ear, his thumb grazing her cheek ever so slightly.

How can I be so full of anger, and then...THIS feeling...at the same time?

He wouldn't say the word to himself. Because he knew that he wasn't being honest with her—could never be honest with her about who and what he really was. It wasn't fair to ask someone to love you without being willing to share everything. In a way, it was a relief to know this could go no farther than flirtation or friendship, and getting someone out of harm's way. This way was far safer.

Then she'd never know that the man sitting beside her in the cab of a semi-truck on the I-65 North was really a monster.

T HEY SHARED A deep-dish 'meat extravaganza' pizza from a tiny mom-and-pop place outside Chicago, but Todd

wouldn't let Margery get dessert no matter how much she begged.

"It's not like I'm watching my figure, Todd! If I were, I never should have signed up to stick with you after that first pancake this morning."

"Trust me, Margie, you don't want to spoil your appetite." She blushed at the nickname, but didn't comment on it as he'd hoped she would.

Instead, she only said, "Does this mean you're finally going to tell me where we're headed?" and lifted her brows towards him expectantly. He let out a breath and smiled.

"Fine, if you want to spoil the surprise. We are going to the Frozen Custard Capital of the World; Milwaukee, Wisconsin." Margery's eyes widened, then narrowed slightly.

"Frozen custard? Isn't that just like ice cream?"

"To the untrained palate, perhaps," Todd said, stroking the stubble on his chin, "but you, Margery, Princess of the Passenger Seat, and Pancake Aficionado, I think you'll be able to tell the difference." Todd saw Margery's face light up with the compliment while simultaneously blushing at his gentle mockery. The flush snuck its way up from beneath the collar of her shirt and spread across her cheeks. Will that blush ever get old?

No. No, I don't think it will.

After she'd regathered her composure she said, "Well then, lead the way, Todd Mackewain! Custard awaits!"

The street lamps were turning on as they crossed the street back to the truck, but Margery's smile was brighter than all of them, and Todd wasn't sure how he'd gone his whole life never knowing how beauty could squeeze your heart just as tightly as the deepest pain.

How joy could feel like fear and loss in the very same moment.

CHAPTER FIVE
Frozen Custard & Promises

MARGERY

"You're kidding me!" Margery exclaimed as they stood in line at the frozen custard counter. "They make a new flavor EVERY DAY?"

"Yep," Todd said, smiling at her in that way that made her feel a little less steady on her feet.

"But you're not here for all those new-fangled flavors-of-the-day."

"I'm not?" she said confused.

"Nope. You're here for *that*." Todd pointed to a sign behind the counter. It read '*Maple Walnut Surprise!*' The sign seemed to shout at them with an overzealous exclamation mark that scared Margery just a little bit.

"Surprise?" she asked, cocking an eyebrow at Todd.

"Hey now, Margery Daniels—when have I ever steered you wrong?"

"When did you learn my last name?" she asked, her lips pursed as she tried not to smile.

"The night I picked you up. Last night...I think it was. I had to pick up your driver's license from the counter at the bar before we left."

"Oh...right..." she said, suddenly embarrassed.

"Plus, you kept using my full name, Todd *Mackewain*, so I figured it was time to try it out. See how it feels to say *your* full name all sassy like."

"And how was it?" She was full-blown smiling now in the slowly moving line up to the custard counter, in the middle of a state she'd never been to, with a man she'd met just the night before. She couldn't even find it in herself to be embarrassed.

"Not as good as the *surprise* is going to be," he said, waggling his eye brows before giving her a wink. Margery flushed and she could have sworn it reached down to where her bare toes peeked out of her comfortably worn sandals. "So," he said, recapturing her attention, "have I ever steered you wrong?"

"Not in the food department," she admitted, thinking of all the delicious things she'd eaten since the night before. They'd reached the counter now, and Todd seemed about to place their order before he turned toward her one final time.

"Do you trust me? Or would you like to order something new-fangled?" he asked, smiling gently even though the teasing gleam was still in his eyes.

And before she could even think about the words, or analyze what they meant, a simple, "Yes," had escaped her lips. "I trust you Todd."

"Good," he said, and turned to place their order.

THE SURPRISE turned out to be little chunks of waffle-cone, broken up and somehow still crisp despite the custard.

The whole concoction was strewn with a maple-infused caramel sauce throughout the maple walnut custard. The crunch of the cone pieces was a perfect balance for the creamy taste of the custard, and Margery was pretty sure it was the best thing she'd ever tasted.

God, I have got to stop saying that!

She'd had friends that had claimed to be foodies before, but Todd was on another level altogether. She imagined his way of picking places to eat earned him lots of praise with whatever female company he chose to keep. And though the old adage states, "the way to *a man's* heart is through his stomach," Margery had always thought this unfair to womenfolk. After all, there wasn't much in life a good meal couldn't at least improve. Folks were bound to have warm feelings toward the one that had given it to them.

"Stunned into silence again?" Todd teased, jarring Margery from her thoughts.

"Do you take all the ladies here?" he burst out suddenly, before she could shove another bite into her mouth. Todd's eyes flashed to hers, and where she expected to see mischief and confident flirtation, she instead saw a neutral face, barely concealing what looked like a deep well of sadness underneath. It was there for only a moment before the confident smirk returned.

"Only the pretty ones," he said, chuckling. She watched as he created the perfect, swirling bite on his spoon and then turned it upside down before putting it in his mouth and sucking it clean.

"I'm sure there have been *plenty* of pretty girls in your life," she said, staring at her sundae.

"No. Not really," he replied. She nearly choked as she digested his words and the serious tone behind them.

"I can't imagine *why!*" she got out before she realized how stupid and possibly sarcastic and insensitive it sounded. She backpedaled. "I mean, you're gorgeous!" She then

turned bright red. *Why won't any words that don't make me sound ridiculous come out of my freaking mouth?*

"Glad to hear you think so," he said, smiling slightly. "At least I have my looks right?" The barely hidden vulnerability in his eyes was slowly killing her.

"I mean, it's not just that! You're charming and funny too, and kind obviously—you've been so kind to me, and to Nelson! You are the kind of guy that rescues puppies and damsels in distress, AND you know where all the good food is. What's not to like?" Todd laughed then, and it was back to the warm sound she'd loved from their drive earlier, chasing away the sadness she'd seen in his eyes a few moments before.

"You've only known me for twenty-four hours, Margery."

"Twenty-Five," she corrected, looking at the clock. "As I recall, you walked into the bar at 7:45 last night, and now it's 8:45," she smiled at him triumphantly.

"And how is it, exactly, that you remembered specifically, what time I walked in last night?"

Crap.

"There's a bell over the door! Isn't there?" She realized she suddenly couldn't remember if there was or not.

"Not that I recall," he said, eyes locked on hers.

"I don't know then..." she said, looking away. She was suddenly very intent on creating the perfect custard bite for herself, "I just...noticed you."

"Because I'm gorgeous."

"Shut UP, Todd!" she said, shoving his elbow. Her face had gone from the light pink of a breakfast radish, to beet red. She could still feel his eyes on her and was determined not to look up into his smugly handsome face until she could regain a little composure.

"Margery," he said after a moment, his voice soft.

"What!?" she said, looking up despite her previous promise to herself. What she saw in his stormy eyes was not

the satisfied look of a man who'd just been given a compliment, but something akin to tenderness.

"I noticed you too," he said almost under his breath, and somehow his whisper skated its way across the table and made gooseflesh broke out across her skin. They locked eyes for a moment then, and Margery suddenly had the sense that Todd was the moon and she was the tide, and she'd be perfectly content to be locked into a push-and-pull rhythm with him for the rest of her days. In a moment that seemed both an instant, and an eternity, Todd's gaze flicked down to her lips.

A sudden chant of "ICE CREAM! ICE CREAM! ICE CREAM!!!" broke the tension, as a young family with three small children passed by their table, the youngest and rowdiest ones, almost knocking into them. Todd laughed and fished his final bite out of his cardboard sundae bowl, smiling at the children, then smiling back at her.

"Actually," Margery said, feigning a snobbish tone of voice, "it's called *Frozen Custard*."

Todd chuckled again, and the sound skittered across her skin and simmered in her bones.

"ALLOW ME TO demonstrate," Todd said, fluffing the twin duvet cover on the lower bunk with the flourish of a magician, before sprawling across her bunk in the cab that night. "IN, the bed—"he said, leaning back with his arm behind his head, his freehand gesturing to his outstretched body. His white shortsleeved undershirt did absolutely nothing to hide his well-formed biceps, and for some reason Margery was finding this very hard not to focus on. "OUT, of the bed," he then said as he swiveled his body to place his feet on the ground and stand up, suddenly only inches away from her.

How have I never noticed how tall he was before? She inhaled

sharply at his nearness but tried to pass it off as a laugh. But breathing in turned out to also be a huge mistake, because all she could think about was how incredible he smelled.

What the hell is wrong with me?

"Well YOU weren't trying to wrestle your way out of the sheets...like they were a...like you were a..."

"Yes, yes, you were thrashing about like a wild cat. I remember. So I have prepared an additional demonstration." He snatched a blanket from his bunk, then lay back down on her bed, covering himself with the blanket. "In cases like these," he said, once again gesturing to himself, "most find it helpful to simply, *pull back* the covers before trying to get into a standing position." His grin in the dim running lights of the cab was like the Cheshire Cat's, but somehow seemed even more dangerous. And Margery had had just about enough of his teasing. Without thinking she yanked the pillow out from beneath his head and smacked him with it.

"YOU. ARE. SUCH. A. SMART. ASS!" she said, as she bludgeoned him repeatedly with the pillow. Todd laughed so hard he seemed unable to make a defense, except to block his face with his forearm, and cross one leg over the other. Her face was beet red again by the time she'd finished exacting her revenge, but she didn't care. She tossed the pillow onto Todd's face and flopped on the edge of the mattress.

"What's wrong with us Todd?" She asked, her voice sounding exhausted to her own ears.

"What do you mean?" he replied, propping himself up on an elbow.

"I mean, you're a great guy. And you're still single. And I...." She swallowed hard before continuing, "I was supposed to be at a hotel right now. Having the pins taken out of my hair by a man who loved me...who...who...I thought loved me. And we were supposed..."

"You were supposed to start your adventure together," he said, his voice full of understanding. She nodded.

"But, I know, you're right, Todd...it's all so clear to me now. He couldn't love me the way I needed him to, and the farther away I get from Alabama, the more I wonder if I ever really loved him at all, either, or if..." She felt the burning in her eyes and her face collapsed into her hands. "I'm a horrible person."

"No, Margery..." Todd shifted behind her, and she felt him gently prying her fingers from her face. "No one who has talked to you for even five minutes could ever think that. You were just...scared. Your mom was sick, and you were afraid of being alone, and she was afraid of that on your behalf, and...you made a mistake." He paused, looking her in the face, and then continued in almost a whisper, "Not everyone is such an honest, open book as you are, Margery. I know I'm not. With you, what you see, is what you get. But some people who look good..." He inhaled sharply, "Some of them are actually monsters."

"You sound like you're speaking from experience," she said. He let out a humorless laugh, and she looked toward him and saw he had drawn himself up to a cross-legged sitting position beside her.

"You could say that. My mom..." he paused, "I never knew my dad. Not really. He was in and out of my life until I was three, when he beat my mom senseless and she got permanent custody of me for good. But after that...it was like she couldn't shake the stain of it. Like the bruises had left a mark on her soul so deep she thought she wasn't worth any more than that. She always left the guys when things turned nasty, but still...she seemed to always gravitate toward the assholes. The ones that beat her down emotionally or made her feel small. And somehow, she never saw that those were the flags—those were the signs it was sure to get ugly again later."

"Todd..." Margery stammered, her throat burning for someone other than herself now, "That's awful."

"Yeah," he said, scrubbing a hand across his face. "It's just another reason I spent all my time at Betsy and Mike's. Even when she was home..." he said, his eyes going distant, "I never quite knew what I was going home to."

"I'm so sorry, Todd," she said, lightly placing a hand on his knee.

"It's okay," he said quickly, as though he were trying to shove all the feelings he'd just unpacked down into the deep, dark hole from whence they came. He ran a hand through his hair and sniffed, glancing at her sidelong at her before looking away.

"It's not okay, Todd," she said. He looked at her, and the pinch in his brow made her long to raise a hand to smooth the furrowed lines away. Instead she curled her fingers into a fist as she repeated, "It's NOT okay."
He nodded slightly like he understood what she meant; like he realized she was someone it was finally okay, to not be okay, with. Like it was okay to look at the raw deal of his life and call it what it was.

"But it will be," he said with a rising conviction.

"Yes," she echoed, "it will be."

"There's nothing wrong with you, Margery," he said softly, peering into her face as though for the first time.

"There's nothing wrong with you, Todd," she replied with a soft smile. "Even if you won't explain to me why you're still single."

"Maybe I just hadn't met a damsel in appropriate levels of distress," he said. "After all, they say that chivalry is dead." She slapped his arm.

"Todd Mackewain, you are incorrigible!"

"And you like it," he said, his chin dimple returning with his smile.

"Yeah," she said, before she could think better of it. "Yeah, I kinda do."

They talked long into the night, about everything and

nothing. In the solidarity that only comes with the mutual sharing of words about their wounds, they found a balm. Margery drifted off, more at ease in the cab of this truck than she'd ever been in her bed next to Shawn. And though the guilt still plagued her through the night, the light of dawn on the following day burned it away, leaving only the song of adventure and potential of second chances humming in its wake.

TODD

TODD AND MARGERY traveled all over, with Todd only taking the contract carrying jobs that took him to his favorite places. They went to Michigan for a pickup at the maple syrup farm that Betsy and Mike favored, and Todd watched, laughing as Margery declared *those* were trees she'd like to hug, running up to one and flinging her arms wide around its trunk. They drove past Lake Michigan one day, and once the fog finally cleared after hours and hours of nothing, Margery gasped at its vastness.

They went to Idaho next. Todd took Margery to Warm River on a day off and they hiked all the way up to where the water poured out at fifty degrees, directly from a rock, all year long. Margery loved the cabin by the old fish hatchery and declared she'd live there if she could. Though, Todd was discovering this woman would say that about almost anywhere that was quaint and cute in some measure. They stopped for tacos at every single authentic Mexican place they saw, but Margery agreed the tacos at Valle Del Sol in Driggs, Idaho were the best. They ate through the stash of trail mix so fast, Margery demanded Todd make more on the road.

He told her he'd have to make a stop home, eventually, to do some laundry, but she simply declared, "Todd Mackewain, when you promise to show a girl the world, you damn

well better do it! Besides, that's what a laundromat is for!" Staring at her luminous form from behind the wheel, her blonde hair loose and curling freely in the breeze, he couldn't possibly argue.

He'd kept a respectful distance these weeks, even though he was dying to know what it would be like to kiss her. But every day they talked, and talked, and talked. They argued about Bluegrass music versus country music. They shared their favorite folk music artists, and their favorite artists to see live. They swapped crazy conspiracy theories and ghost stories and Todd revealed his middle name was Rollins, which made Margery laugh for a full twenty minutes, even though it wasn't that funny, and hers was revealed to be way worse: *Petunia*. They talked about everything, and every vestige of reserve Todd had attempted that first day to keep her at arms length, was obliterated. He found, that even though he knew it wasn't fair, *he wanted to be known* by this woman. As much as he could be. For as long as she'd let him.

They were just pulling in to Jackson Hole, Wyoming when Margery received a phone call.

"It's my mom, I'll just take this real quick and then we can go to dinner," she said, hopping out of the cab where they'd parked at a truck stop on the outskirts of town. She'd talked with her mom plenty of times before, but something told Todd this wasn't any ordinary call. It was a sense as unexplainable as his gift, but no less *real*; an ominous foreboding crawling through the cab like a shadow. A moment later, his suspicions were confirmed when Margery climbed back into the seat, her face not pink as it usually was in a moment of overwhelm or excitement; but as pale as Todd had seen it in his vision of her death.

"Margery!" he said, immediately reaching for her to check if she were somehow wounded. "What's wrong?"

"That was...that was the hospital," Margery said. "My mom...she....she collapsed at home this morning. Her neigh-

bor, Susan, found her a few hours ago and rushed her in…" Her face collapsed into an ugly sob that tore Todd's heart to shreds. "She's still unconscious."

"Which hospital?" Todd asked quickly, getting out of his seat and buckling her seatbelt around her before climbing back in his own seat.

"D.W. Memorial," she said numbly.

"Alright," he said, setting the trucks navigation before turning to face her. He cradled the back of her neck and pulled her forehead against his for a moment, stroking his thumb across her cold cheek. "It's not okay Margery," he whispered, "but it's going to be. I promise."

"You can't promise that Todd," she said, frozen, her eyes barely blinking even as the tears built in her eyes, then fell. "No one knows what the future holds."
His frustration was all the fuel he needed as he pulled back out of the truck stop and onto the highway again.

"Well maybe it's about damn time someone tried," he said, anguished. He slid his hand from her neck down to her hand and placed it gently on the console between them, as if he could hold her together—as if he could hold *them* together—as he turned toward the road that would take them back.

Back to Brewton, Alabama—and all that awaited Margery there.

CHAPTER SIX
Back to Brewton

TODD

IT WAS AGONY to keep driving. Todd now realized that these past few weeks had been a dream of sorts. He'd floated through them with Margery at his side; showing her sights, bringing her to the best spots to eat, laughing and arguing with her every mile in between. And now, as though another semi-truck was blaring its horn at him, the headlights slicing through his windshield in warning, the dream was ending. He knew he was barreling toward a head-on collision with everything he'd tried to keep hidden—every part of himself he wished he could be rid of.

He looked over again at the woman sitting next to him. Her hair was pulled into a loose ponytail from earlier, but several escaped strands had refused containment and now found themselves floating in the breeze of Margery's breath. She was staring straight out through the windshield, and Todd wondered if she were even blinking. He looked down at the waters they'd refilled three hours ago at the last rest stop, and saw hers was nearly full.

"You should drink something," Todd said gently. The old Margery would have been startled from her reverie by his voice, but this Margery only turned her face slowly toward him, a look of concentration and vague confusion on her face.

"What?" she croaked.

"Water. Drink some water, Margery. You need to stay hydrated." She moved then, in what seemed like slow motion, bringing the straw cup to her lips and taking a small sip. Then, as though realizing she'd been desperately thirsty this entire time, she took another, longer sip, before setting the cup back in its holder.

"Are you hungry at all? Do you need some more trail mix?" he asked, reaching for the latch on the center console.

"I'm fine," she said. Her voice was detached and floating—like a balloon let loose to explore the atmosphere.

Todd knew that was a lie from the pit of hell, but he didn't call her on it. He knew how it felt to live on the edge of "fine". How sometimes, "fine", was the only blanket you could wrap around yourself to keep out the chill of a life that had frozen over.

It was agony. But Todd kept driving.

MARGERY

I CAN'T BELIEVE I left her. I can't believe I left her. I can't

believe I left her. I can't believe I left her. I can't believe I left her. I can't believe I left her. I can't believe I left her. I can't believe I left her. I can't believe I left her. I can't believe I left her. I can't believe I left her. I can't believe I left her. I can't believe I left her. I can't believe I left her. I can't believe I left her. I can't believe I left her. I can't believe I left her. I can't believe I left her.

I can't believe I left.

TODD

THEY MADE IT through Denver by 2:00 AM. They grabbed a quick breakfast in Wichita at 9:00 AM. When they stopped for fuel, Todd excused himself from the eerily quiet cab for a moment to make a phone call.

"Todd? Is everything alright?" Betsy asked, answering nearly on the first ring.

"I'm..." Todd stumbled...

"TODD? Were you in a wreck? What hospital are you at? Let me just grab my purse and I'll..."

"No, it's not me, Betsy," Todd said quickly, "I'm fine. It's just... we're headed back to Alabama." There was a silence on the other end of the phone. "Margery's Mom is in the hospital."

"Oh...oh, Todd. I'm so sorry. Poor thing. How's Margery holding up?"

"She's..." Todd glanced toward the cab of the truck where he knew Margery was leaning her head against the window, staring out at nothing, just as she had been for nearly their entire drive back to Brewton. "She's...I don't know. She's hardly spoken a word since she got off the phone with the hospital last night."

"She's probably in shock, honey," Betsy said sympathetically. "Just keep taking care of what needs taking care of Todd. You've always been a good boy. You'll know what to do

when the time comes."

He smiled at her voice, her tone, her words—for a moment feeling like he was the young man who used to spend all his spare time in Betsy's kitchen; like the world was as simple as good food, and friends who felt like family. He'd felt that again with Margery these past few weeks...but now?

"Thanks," he said at last, "I will. Love you, Bets."

"Love you too, honey."

Todd hung up the phone and took a deep breath, running a hand through his disheveled hair. A few minutes later, he climbed back into the truck and gently rubbed Margery's knee to get her attention.

"I brought you some hot tea," he said. "It's a lavender chamomile. It's supposed to be soothing or something," he added, furrowing his brows and squinting at little tag on the tea bag as if it held all the answers to the universe.

If only.

Margery turned slowly to face him.

"Thanks." Her voice was hoarse and tired.

"We'll need to stop in a few hours to sleep a bit before we keep going. I'll be good with four hours or so...but are you sure you don't want me to just drive you to the nearest airport? I'll buy you a ticket..."

"No," Margery said, stopping him with her hand extended, her face somehow even paler than it had been a moment before. A second later, she dropped her hand again as though she were weak. "I don't want to get in one of those...those...death capsules." She shook her head vehemently; the motion more than Todd had seen her do in over twelve hours. "I need to get to my mother in one piece. My Aunt Melba is there now anyway. She said she'll let me know if there's any news."

I'd never have guessed, she's afraid of flying. Todd wished he could tease her about this sudden revelation but the fear and anguish in her voice brooked no argument, teasing or otherwise. The lump in his throat transformed into a tightness in his chest, and he rubbed the heel of his hand against the ache as if doing so would ease it.

"And has there been any?" Todd asked gently.

"Any what?" Margery looked at him again, confusion stamping her forehead and darkening her pale blue eyes.

"Any news?"

"The doctors are running tests…" she said, tugging at the ends of her ponytail. "But she's still unconscious."

"What do you need, Margery? Just tell me," he said softly. He reached out to pat her knee again, but the moment his hand landed there, she covered it with hers. The silence that stretched between them was taut with all that was unspeakable, and all that still remained unsaid.

"Just…just drive, Todd," Margery said at last.

"Yes ma'am," Todd said with a slight curl at the corner of his mouth, but the words fell flat even to his own ears. He knew that there was no charm that could help this situation. No.

The only thing that could help Margery now, would be if Todd could tell Margery her mother was going to live. *But I won't know until I look her in the eyes.*

For most of his life, Todd had seen himself as a harbinger of death. But Margery had changed things. And maybe—just maybe—it was time to see his gift, as a gift after all.

MARGERY

MARGERY'S WORLD had expanded to the size of galaxies over the course of the past three weeks, and then narrowed again to a pinhole in the blink of an eye. She knew they were traveling through places she'd longed for years to see, but the Rocky Mountains of Colorado held no sway in the face of her fears about her mother. The big skies of the plains failed to awe her. She didn't even remember what, or if, she ate, though she knew Todd was stopping at regular intervals to feed her.

Todd.

Todd's presence was both a source of guilt, and some-how...an incredible comfort. She felt so guilty she'd left her mom in the face of all that was happening. And yet, she was so glad to have him here with her.

How can three short weeks do this to a person? How can Todd suddenly be the only person I want by my side when it feels like my whole world is falling apart?

Her doubts and questions plagued her during the long miles back to Alabama. Thankfully, since the morning after she'd heard her mother had been admitted to D.W. Memorial, her Aunt Melba had been by her mother's side, arrived and Margery was able to receive regular updates even though she was still miles away. Or rather, *non-updates.*

Her mother's condition hadn't changed since she'd been found unconscious in her home. The doctors said it looked as though she'd taken a bit of a minor blow to the back of her head when she fell, and they were encouraging, telling the family that the swelling on her brain was likely causing a temporary coma. Meanwhile, they were looking into the reason behind why she'd fallen in the first place.

What if the cancer's back? What if it's spread and we didn't know it? What if, while I've been playing roadtrip romance with Todd after running away from my wedding and all my responsibili-ties back in Brewton...what if she dies?

The thoughts haunted her. Night, into day, and into night, again.They stopped for only a few hours so Todd could sleep, but Margery just stared at the bunk above hers, unable to get more than a few fitful moments of rest before Todd's alarm went off and they started off again.

"If we keep this pace, we'll be there by tomorrow af-ternoon," Todd said as he climbed back behind the wheel. His hair was still damp from the quick shower he'd taken after his four-hour nap at the truck stop. Margery couldn't remember when she'd last seen his chin dimple that had driven her so crazy these past few weeks, and she found

herself wishing he'd look her way.

"I never thanked you, Todd."

"Thanked me? For what?"

"For..." she gestured aimlessly, "for all of it. For dropping everything to drive me back. Oh, SHIT! You don't even have a load right now do you?"

"I told the dispatcher I needed a few days off after that last drop in Jackson Hole. I've hardly ever taken any vacation time since I started working with this company five years ago."

"Oh Todd...I'm so sorry. What a waste."

"Waste?"

"Of your vacation time. You should be, like, tanning your chin dimple on a beach right now with all the beautiful bikini-clad people, and instead you're driving the most morose person across the country to...to a hospital." Her voice choked on the last words as she stared at the fading light through the windshield as they headed east.

"You really are obsessed with my chin dimple, aren't you?" Todd said, smiling slightly and making it appear behind his unusually thick stubble. His smile quickly faded. "It's not a waste, Margery." Todd turned his face toward her and smiled sadly. "Every mile traveled with you is...it's been a damn honor."

Margery wasn't sure she'd ever heard anything more beautifully sincere, yet simultaneously heartbreaking. Suddenly her heart was sinking in her chest for a completely different reason.

"Why does it sound like you're saying goodbye without saying it?" she asked before she could think better of it.

I can't do this alone.

Todd paled for a moment, his hands flexing slightly on the steering wheel before he said, "I'm not. I'm here, Margery. Or there. I'm wherever you are. For as long as you want me."

The lump rose in her throat again at his honest confession, and finally—finally—in the face of all the despair and the fear of sudden loss, she remembered that so few hon-est-to-goodness things actually happened in life.

And when they do, you need to snatch them up before they blow away like dandelion wishes.

"I can't imagine a future where I don't want you, Todd," she said, and meant it.

So much had changed in these past weeks—*she had changed*. She'd become the version of herself that laughed freely and took risks. She'd never felt more fully *herself*. Between them on the center console of the truck, she stretched out her arm and laid her palm face up.

And Todd, without hesitation, took her soft hand in his own.

TODD

I AM SO completely fucked.
Todd drove through another night, and into the brightness of another day; the day he knew would be his last spent with Margery. They drove the highways and ducked into the side streets for edible breakfasts and lunches when they needed them, but just as he'd told Margery they would, they arrived at D.W. Memorial Hospital in the early afternoon.

"Do you want me to drop you off?"

"You're not coming?" Margery looked panicked.

"No, of course I'm coming, Margie, I just wasn't sure if you wanted to get a head start." He gave her a smile he hoped looked reassuring.

"No, I'm okay. Let's walk in together." She squeezed his hand again where he'd kept it on the center console almost continually since she'd extended hers. He knew he'd be in

a world of trouble with his own heart later, but he couldn't bear to withhold a single comfort from hers.

For as long as you want me.

Thankfully, this small-town hospital had enough nearby side streets of a decent width, and he was able to park the big rig within fairly easy walking distance. When they entered the sterile building, a large dark-skinned woman behind the welcome desk recognized Margery and immediately welcomed her with open arms.

"Margery! It's good to see you, honey, I'm so glad you made it. And just in time, too!" she said, wrapping maternal arms around the trembling Margery. *She looks exhausted. Has she gotten any sleep since we left Wyoming?*

"Hey, Sylvie...it's good to see you too. In time...in time for what?" Margery asked, suddenly stricken.

"Your Mama's awake! Come on now! Best not keep her waiting!" Margery turned a fearful face toward Todd, and he tried again with his attempt at a reassuring smile, though he wasn't sure he was any good at them. Then they followed a surprisingly fast Sylvie, silently down the hall.

The room where Margery's mother, Helen, was staying was painted an unexpected rose pink that Todd almost thought he could smell. *No wait, it's because of all the flowers.* On nearly every surface of the room, there were bouquets upon bouquets of flowers. But the woman in the bed was more beautiful than any of them as she turned her face toward where they stood in the doorway.

"Baby girl," she cooed, and Margery went running into her arms.

"Careful now!" said Sylvie, fussing about the IV lines, and the covers in Helen's lap. "The woman just woke from a coma, and I don't want nothing putting her back into one again." Margery just leaned into her mother and held her tight.

"Thanks, Sylvie," Margery said almost breathlessly, pull-

ing away from her mother.

"Is this the young man you've told me so much about?" Helen asked.

"Yes Mama...this is Todd." Margery gestured towards him, smiling tenderly.

"Ma'am." Todd said, nodding to her from where he stood in the doorway. Helen's eyes were clear and as sharp as a winter's sky when Todd finally raised his gaze to hers.

CHAPTER SEVEN
The Truth Comes Out

TODD

Fᴏʀ ᴀ ᴍᴏᴍᴇɴᴛ the hospital room faded from sight and was replaced by a different room entirely.

Helen lay quiet in her bed; not the hospital bed, but in a room of yellow wallpaper dotted with tiny rosebuds, and on a small wrought iron bed frame. From her grey hair and the way her skin had begun to resemble crumpled paper, Todd knew this scene would hapen decades from now. He glanced up and saw another woman there, middle-aged with fine lines around her eyes that turned up at the corners from years of laughter and smiling. She was holding the elderly woman's hand as the older woman took in her last rattling breath. The tears began to fall from the younger woman's eyes, landing softly on the floral bedspread.

"I'll see you later, Mama," she said. "I'll see you."
Helen was gone then. But before the vision ended, the younger

woman looked up, and straight into Todd's eyes, her blonde hair streaked with bits of grey, and gave a small, tenuous smile, as though she could see him—as though he were somehow really there.

The vision ended as abruptly as they always did, and Todd was thrust back into the hospital room with Margery and Helen, just as Sylvie was saying something about the doctor coming in a few minutes to give test results.

"I can give you both some privacy," Todd said, backing out the door awkwardly before Margery's voice stopped him in his tracks.

"Wait! Todd! Don't go."

She looked at him with those clear blue eyes. She'd tossed her hair into a messy topknot that morning and she was again wearing that bedazzled 'TENNESEE' shirt they'd bought their first day together, and Todd couldn't help but smile. She was the most beautiful woman he had ever seen.

"I'll be right back. I promise."

Before she could make him reconsider once again, he left the room and walked down to the nearest coffee kiosk. He needed a moment to breathe; to collect himself and to process what he'd just seen. The kiosk was only down the hall and around the corner past the nurses' station, but it was far enough for Todd to breathe more deeply than he had since that first time he'd looked into Margery's eyes…and seen her untimely murder.

*I did it. I actually did it. Gran always said the visions didn't show a future that was always certain, but showed the probabilities of possibilities. She always said she gave the gift to me because I had more imagination than Mom…but I never imagined this. All these years, I never imagined I could **actually change** things.*

He kept turning the thoughts around and around in his mind as he fumbled with the waxed paper cups at the coffee kiosk and filled one for Margery, being sure to add a healthy

dose of creamer. Then he filled his own to the brim with steaming, black coffee—which was sure to taste horrid, but he desperately needed it anyway. He'd hardly slept since the hospital had called Margery three days ago, and his eyes felt gritty like they always did when he pushed himself too hard trying to deliver a shipment ahead of schedule. Todd held the cup lightly in his calloused hand for a moment before taking a sip. *Yep. Tastes like dirt.* But he kept drinking as the thoughts repeated over and over in his head.

I did it. I really did it.

A few minutes later, Todd approached Helen's hospital room door with a lightness in his step he hadn't experienced during his entire adult life, but before he could step over the threshold, he heard Margery's previously serene voice raised in a fever pitch.

"What do you mean the cancer *might* be back?" Another, quieter male voice spoke, but Todd was too stunned to hear what he said.

"You've been running all these tests, for DAYS, in here, and you don't know for sure?" There was more low, garbled speaking. Todd leaned in to try to hear without being seen, but the man didn't seem capable of speaking above a near whisper. Margery heard well enough, though. That was painfully clear.

"Yes, you'd better go and look at your numbers again, and come back when you know what the hell you're talking about!" Margery was practically shouting, and Todd's palms turned to ice against the hot cups of coffee in his hands. He waited at the door for a short, balding man in a white coat to shuffle his way out of the room.

"Excuse me," he said, to Todd, his eyes shifting to look at his feet as he walked past Todd and down the hall. Todd then stepped back into the room. His heart collapsed in his chest when he saw Margery's shoulders shaking with sobs as she leaned over her mother's lap. The anger she'd shown just a

moment before had blown itself out, and now, this woman who had suddenly come to mean everything to him was crying. He knew what she was afraid of. It was a fear that haunted his every step—his every glance into a stranger's eyes: She was afraid death was just around the corner. And only Todd could tell her any different.

Helen absently stroked Margery's hair as he entered the room, but said nothing, her lips pressed tightly together. Todd saw in her face the determined look of a mother who had spent her life working herself to the bone to give her child everything. Though he'd only just met her, Todd could see Helen was a fighter—and she wasn't about to stop fighting now.

So that's where Margery gets it from.

"Margery?" Todd called to her and she slowly lifted her head to look at him. Her face was pale and drawn as it had been on the drive back to the hospital, and her eyes held both deep sorrow and unrelenting anger. "Can I talk to you for a minute...out in the hall?" He gave an apologetic smile to Helen, whose lips tipped up in gratitude and understanding.

"Go. Go. I'm not going anywhere, darling." Helen brushed a stray tear from Margery's cheek and then wiped at her own eyes. Margery sniffed and slowly rose to her feet and approached the door. He tucked one of the coffe cups in the crook of his elbow and arranged the other in his left hand. When Margery was in reach, Todd brushed a comforting hand down her arm and gently guided her to a short row of uncomfortable plastic chairs a little way down the hall. He handed her the cup of coffee he'd loaded with cream and they sat.

"Margery, there's something I need to tell you." Margery sipped from her coffee and stared at him, her eyes almost vacant, as though she were too tired to make facial expressions anymore.

"I'm not sure now is the best time for more bad news," she said, staring at the stray splash of coffee on the white plastic lid of her cup as if it might hold all the certainties of the uncertain universe.

"Well, it's not bad news exactly. It's sort of good actually."

"What do you mean by 'sort of good'?" She raised her brows at him incredulously, and Todd wished he could lean forward and kiss the pucker in the middle of her forehead that came with the motion, but he knew this was not the right moment.

He breathed out a long sigh and began again, "I'm sorry, Margie, I started this all wrong. I need to tell you something, but it might seem totally unbelievable, so you'll need to just...I don't know...do what they say in the theatre world and suspend your disbelief for a minute." Margery pursed her lips, considering, then took a deep breath.

"Okay," she said, "Consider my disbelief temporarily suspended." She took another sip of her coffee.
This is it.

"Your mom doesn't have cancer. Or...or if she does, she doesn't die from it at least. In fact, she doesn't die for a long, long time." He said the words softly, like a secret. Like a sweet nothing. Like the only gift he had to give this woman he cared so much about. He'd never once told someone what he saw in his visions, not since the day he'd first received the gift and his grandmother had asked him quietly, "Do I have to wait long?" and the young Todd had shaken his head.

For most, knowing how the end would come would cause more terror than comfort. But his Gran had lived her whole life with this same gift—seeing death in the eyes of every stranger, before ever getting to know them in life. She knew there were good and bad ways to die. And hers had been as good a way as any.

MARGERY

Margery's head was spinning with the words Todd had just said.

"What?" Margery's question sounded less quizzical and more exclamatory. *What the hell is he talking about? How could he possibly know she doesn't die...or know when she's going to die?*

"She doesn't die. I mean she dies eventually—we all do—but not yet, and not from this. She lives to be an old, gray woman—a couple decades more at least, I'd guess...and you're with her when she goes, and she's peaceful and held, and loved. It's...it's the most beautiful ending one could hope for in a world where death exists." Margery saw a sheen of unshed tears welling in his eyes, and she couldn't tell if they were tears for the horror of all he'd seen, or if they were somehow for the beauty of the moment her mother would go to glory, with Margery there to hold her hand.

She needed to say something. But all she could come up with was, "Todd...you're freaking me out. How could you possibly know any of that?" She was staring at him hard now, as though he were a puzzle she didn't remember buying, and certainly didn't remember dumping out.

"I'm not just a trucker, Margery. That's what I'm trying to tell you." Margery felt all the blood draining from her face. *He must be crazy. He's lost his mind from too many road fumes and truck stop snacks.* Her mouth opened to say something sensible in the midst of all this nonsense, but Todd continued.

"When I was eight, before my gran passed away, she gave me this...gift. At least, she always called it a gift. But I never saw it that way until I met you. And that night—the night we met—I was so angry at what I'd seen, and I did something a little bit crazy, because after all these years of seeing what I see, and feeling cursed by it, I thought, *"What*

if? What if I could change things?"

"Change what, Todd?" Margery's voice sounded small and tinny to her own ears.

"The future."
Todd's eyes were on hers now, and something burned in their depths; something like anger…and hope.

"You can see the future?" She covered her mouth with a hand, as though she could keep the insanity of the words she was speaking from escaping out into the world as she'd always known it: The world where the Supernatural was reserved for myths and Sunday School.

"I see what my Gran called 'the probabilities of possibilities'. And It's not like a sure thing, but the long and the short of it is, the first time I look into someone's eyes…" His gaze flicked up to hers beneath his dark lashes. "I see the moment of their death."

Margery was stunned into silence then, imagining what it would be like to see death in the eyes of every stranger. Despite his charm and the obvious love of Betsy and Mike, Todd had always seemed to turn inward when they were around new people. He would shift uneasily on his feet and avoided eye contact often, especially with those he didn't know. All of a sudden it made sense: his preference for restaurants and hole-in-the-wall places where he knew the owners, or had at least previously been before. His love of life on the road. The seeming inability to maintain any kind of romantic relationship. His lack of close friendships with anyone other than those he spoke to on the radio. As though she were watching a tragic movie, she imagined what Todd's life must have been like all these years before they met; the weight of unavoidable death constantly pressing down on his shoulders. Then with a start, something occurred to her.

"But, Todd…you looked into my eyes," she said at last.

"Yes," he said, "I did." He paused, and the look in his eyes was begging her to understand. "I hadn't planned on it. I

noticed you when I first came in to the bar that night, and you were so radiant and happy and I knew I did not want to see what happened next. But then you slipped and fell, and before I knew it I was there, holding you, watching as…" He tore his eyes away from hers, his throat bobbing with emotion. "Watching as the light and laughter left your eyes. And I couldn't do it any more, Margery."

"Couldn't do what, Todd?" Her heart was hammering in her chest as she stared at the side of his face. The shadows of each hair on his unshaved face were thrown into stark relief by the godless fluorescence of the hospital lighting. Somewhere, she heard a heart monitor beeping. Down the hall a doctor being being paged. A nurse walked by in 'Puppy Love' scrubs, placing updated charts next to patient rooms. A teenage boy rolled by in a wheel chair. Todd studiously avoided their gazes, even as he finally lifted his eyes to Margery's once more. When he finally spoke, there was an edge of rage and desperation in his tone that Margery had never heard before.

"I couldn't just stand by and let him kill you."

TODD

MARGERY WAS looking at him like he'd grown a second head…or horns…or maybe both.

"Oh, my God, Todd…what are you saying?" Her eyes were wide with horror and shock.

"You don't want to hear it, Margery."

"Like HELL, I don't," she spat.

"It's not good to hear the things I see, Margie. Trust me on this."

"Trust ME when I tell you, you have kept enough secrets from me, Todd Mackewain, and now it's time to come all the

way clean, or not at all." Her fear had turned to an unwieldy live wire, and her eyes seemed to dance with a dangerous spark. *The whole truth it is, then.*

"Fine," he bit out, his anger getting the upper hand on the good judgment that was still screaming at him to keep his mouth shut. "Do you really want to know what I saw when I looked into your eyes that night?"

"Yes, I really do." Her face was red with agitation.

"I saw you in your wedding dress, a necklace of bruises around your neck, and the light fading from your eyes as a pool of blood seeped out from beneath your hair. And I saw..." He paused for a moment, trying to catch his breath at the memories. "And I saw a man's hands—*his hands*—with a brand new wedding band on that left-hand ring finger. And *I knew.*" He paused again before adding, "I knew that if I didn't do something crazy—something against all the rules—that by the end of the following day, you'd be dead. You were a stranger to me, but you had so much laughter in your eyes, and the thought of that being snuffed out was... it was unbearable." He looked up into Margery's eyes and saw the truth of his words beginning to sink into their blue depths.

"Shawn was...Shawn would have killed me on our wedding night?" She barely got the words past her lips. "But WHY?"

"I don't know that. The visions only show me glimpses; snippets of what the future is currently shaping up to be. The trajectory is set by so many factors I am not privy to. But the long story short is that night...I broke all the rules I've lived my whole life by, and for this moment right here..." He turned toward Margery and ran his hand on the inside of her wrist, feeling her strong pulse with his fingertips. "I'd do it again."

"Do what, exactly Todd? What rules did you break? Why is helping someone against the rules?"

"I never knew if it was exactly, but Betsy and Mike…Now don't think less of them alright? But you know they practically raised me after my gran passed, and they've always been a little more old school about the future, like 'you have no business mucking about with fate.'" He paused, his face looking stricken, then continued, "When I was ten I had this friend…and when we first met I saw he was going to get hit by a car one day while crossing the school's crosswalk. So every day that year, I stuck by him like glue. I walked with him across the crosswalk every day to and from school, and sure enough, the day that a car came out of nowhere, I was able to yank him back."

"That's amazing Todd! You could do so much…"Margery's mouth opened in an 'O' as she spoke in hushed awe.

"That's not the end of the story, Margery."

"What? What do you mean?"

"He died in a car crash two years later. His mother with him."

"Oh….oh God…"Margery said under her breath.

"Betsy and Mike…you know they're good people, but they took that as confirmationI shouldn't be trying to change things. I shouldn't be messing with fate, or the divine order, or the universe…whatever you want to call it. 'What happens is meant to happen,' they said. It was for the best to leave well enough alone. But they never had to live under the weight of seeing what I see…*of knowing what I know.*"

"That must have been awful."

Todd saw the sincere grief in her eyes, and he hoped maybe, just maybe, he wasn't actually about to lose the one good thing he had going in his life. But she'd told him to come clean, and it was time he did.

"You asked me for the whole truth, Margery, and I'm going to give it to you. If that's still what you want."

"Of course that's what I want, Todd. Honesty is the foundation of any trusting relationship." She smiled gently

at him, as though she were teasing him. But he knew she wasn't. It was only to soften the bite of her words; the threat of what would happen to them if he continued keeping secrets.

"Do you remember the morning you woke up in the cab of my truck?"

"How could I forget it? The night before—half of it seems to have packed its bags and taken off for good—but that morning..." She trailed off before adding, "I remember."

"Do you remember how you asked me if I had kidnapped you?" He peered up into her face, his fingers still idly tracing the pulse point in her wrist.

"Yes..."

"And I told you, that you had asked me to 'just drive?'" He turned her palm face up and began tracing the lines there.

"Yes...because I was having second thoughts. Seems I was smarter than Shawn gave me credit for." She smiled at him, but Todd's hands stilled as her cupped her hands between his own.

"Margery, I lied."

"What?"

"I lied. You didn't tell me to just drive. You weren't having second thoughts, at least, not enough that you'd tell a complete stranger to take you with him out of town."

"Todd, what are you saying?"

"I'm saying I committed one wrong in order to make something else right. That night we drove out of Brewton...*I did kidnap you.* All you said before you passed out was that you needed a ride home. Nothing about second thoughts. You didn't tell me to drive. I made the decision to leave town with you all by myself. But you were drunk, and I'd seen what was coming in your eyes so I took the chance you would believe me." His voice was rising in desperation now, and his throat felt like it was closing as he remembered exactly what he'd seen when he first looked into Margery's

eyes. "I just had to get you away." But just as these final words—this final raw confession—left his lips, Margery pulled her hand away from his.

"You...you *kidnapped me?*"

"Margery..."

"Not telling me about the gift is one thing. That's your story to tell and your story alone. *But now I find out that you kidnapped me, and then lied about it?*"

"Margery, until you, my life was either desperate loneliness or witnessing death after death in the eyes of strangers. But then I met you, and in a moment, everything changed. I couldn't just let him kill you; that much was clear. But it wasn't until we started heading North, I realized, maybe I wasn't only here for you...maybe you were here for me too. Maybe I didn't have to live a life of lonely existence, just driving place to place, avoiding any close connection with people, because nothing hurts worse than loving someone and..." He trailed off.

"And what, Todd?" Her voice was tight and tense, but he plowed ahead anyway.

"And knowing you're about to lose them."

MARGERY

BETRAYAL BURNED raw, like acid in her throat. She stared down at her coffee cup and tried to digest it all.

The gift.

The lie.

The hope that her mother would live.

The truth that she'd been living in a fantasy with a man she barely knew, and now, could no longer trust.

She didn't know how to be, in this moment. She could barely

remember how to breathe. She needed space. And time. It was all too much. Much too much.

"Todd, I think you should go."

"Sure, sure. I understand you need time to process." He scrubbed a hand down his face. "I can go and grab you guys some lunch while I'm out. Do you want something from…"

"No, Todd." Margery held up a hand in final resolution, her body making decisions for her while her mind continued to reel. "As hungry as I am, I don't think even the most orgasmic burger in the world could make this better right now." Her face was set like a flint, but her eyes were heavy with betrayal and hurt.

"What…" He sat there, looking stunned. His brow furrowed in a way she'd often found adorable, but now made her see red. "What are you saying?"

"I'm telling you to go, Todd. Just go. Just drive. Go make Francine the happiest truck dispatcher in the world and pick her up some of those chicken wings you were pointing out twenty minutes ago. I don't care. You need to…" Her face burned in the way that told her it was going red and blotchy in patches, and her eyes began to sting.

"Francine's out at headquarters in Ohio…Margery…"

"I don't want to hear it, Todd! You have visions. You have a gift. You're the harbinger of death, but you saved my life. I'm grateful to you for all you've done but…" She took a shaky breath, tucking her free hand beneath her armpit, and trying to keep the cup of coffee in her other hand from betraying how she'd begun to shake. "But we've been living a fantasy. A romantic roadtrip adventure, and it was all based on a lie. A lie *you told me*. Can't you see, we can't go on like this?" It felt like her heart was tearing in two to say those words, but they had to be said. She'd lived with one morally grey man before. What good was it to trade him in for another?

"Okay," Todd said, slowly coming to a standing position, "I understand. But can I just say one last thing Margery?"

"One last thing," she said, her voice wavering between wobbling with tears and a vacant hollowness that bounced off her bones.

"I'm sorry I lied to you, but after seeing you with your mom today..." He trailed off. "If I had to choose—your life, or your love—I'd choose your life every time. *You are a star, Margery.* The damn brightest light in the dark I've ever seen. And the world is a much better place with you in it. Trust me. I've seen the alternative."

With that, Todd turned from where she sat in the hallway and beneath the flickering lights of the hospital fluorescents, Margery watched as the man she loved walked away.

CHAPTER EIGHT
Danger & Delivery

MARGERY

Margery returned to her mother's hospital room, a numb expression on her normally animated face.

"What is it, sweetheart?" her mother asked almost immediately. "Where's that nice young man? Todd, was it?" At the sound of his name Margery's eyes whipped to her mother's and she let out a sudden shuddering breath.

"Let there be no secrets between us anymore Mama," Margery said. And she told her mother everything: about the roadtrip with Todd, the way he picked out all the best foods, about the way Shawn had treated her behind closed doors, and about how relieved she'd been to cancel the wedding. She talked about the damn dimple in Todd's chin that made him so irresistible. Finally, she told her what Todd had only just revealed—the gift he'd shared and the lie he'd told.

"But the upshot is…you're going to be okay, Mama," she said softly at last, "for a long, long time."

"But, Margery…" her Mother said, "what about you? Will you be okay?"

"Yes," she said, raising her head, giving a small smile she could only hope looked sincere. "I will be. I just need to order us some lunch. There's a great new wing place in town that I hear has good reviews. I know how you love your Buffalo sauce. I'll call in an order."

Margery pulled out her phone and walked into the hall. Without even thinking, her fingers automatically opened up the messages between her and Todd from a few days earlier. He'd pulled into a truck stop with a giant cinnamon roll for the logo and had run in to grab them some snacks to tide them over until dinner.

TODD: So, no trail mix, then?

MARGERY: NO. You've ruined me for all other trail mixes.

TODD: Granola?

MARGERY: Is it as good as yours?

TODD: Probably not.

MARGERY: Pass.

TODD: Corn Nuts?

MARGERY: Do they have the ranch ones?

TODD: No, only Chile Picante and Original.

MARGERY: Pass.

TODD: You told me you were starving.

MARGERY: I am!

TODD: Then what do you want?

MARGERY: What about one of those giant cinnamon rolls? Like on the SIGN!

TODD: You want a cinnamon roll at 3:30 PM?

MARGERY: Todd, there is no wrong time for butter-filled pastries.

TODD: Oh shit, you're right. One giant cinnamon roll it is.

Her face flushed reading the silly banter, and she leaned back against the hospital wall as a pair of nurses walked by, their gazes flicking to her as their heads bowed together in quiet conversation. *And so, the gossip train begins.* She missed the anonymity of roadtrip life already.

How could this have been only a few days ago? And how is it that I miss him this much when he's been gone all of five minutes? Without her consent, her mind brought up pictures of Todd's mischievous eyes, his pleasing smile, and the way his laugh quirked up the left corner of his mouth slightly more than the right. She thought about the way he'd mocked her and teased her to the point of her blushing, as though that was what he was waiting for when he did it. She thought of how he'd grabbed her hands at that first breakfast and told her how Shawn's poor attempts at love and care were not enough. She thought about how safe she'd felt traveling around the country with a man she'd only just met, sharing the beauty of rivers and lakes, taco stands, and mom-and-pop ice cream shops, with extra 'p's and 'e's thrown on the

end for good measure.

She thought about Todd's earnest gaze as he'd told her about his gift, and the hope that had sparked in her chest when he told her that her mother was going to live.

And then she thought of the way he'd looked at her when she'd told him to go—as though it were ripping him in half to walk away from her, even though running was all he'd ever done his entire adult life.

He lied to you, remember? Who knows how much of that was.… was even real.

She shook her head and straightened up. Then she took a deep breath and placed an order for buffalo chicken wings with extra blue cheese dressing on the side.

TODD

TODD STARED into the amber liquid of his rocks glass, watching the swirls and whirls caused by the centrifugal force, as his wrist rotated—around, and around, and around. It seemed like that was how his life had always been too. Hope and despair swirling around the edges, while he tried to live in the shallow middle; never hoping, never longing, never daring for more. He'd called himself "content", but what he'd really been was wildly afraid—a coward.

And now it was time to pay the piper. Now, he was swept up into the tornado of uncertainty; the agony of wanting what could, perhaps, never be his. The ache of it made him feel human. And the pain of it? That made him feel alive.

And yet, here he was, numbing some of that double-edged sorrow with a glass of whiskey in the bar where he and Margery had met only a few weeks before. He told himself he was acclimating—planning his next move and deciding where the next adventure lay—now that Margery

had told him to go.

But really, he was waiting. Lingering. Biding his time and staying close.

It was quiet in the bar, with barely a patron other than himself, and Todd realized that he'd lost track of the days while driving with Margery—even more so in their rush to return to Brewton. It was a Tuesday at 2pm, and the large, slightly balding barman named Stan, who was not the one who'd been here the first night he'd walked in, was bored with no one to talk to except a kitchen staff member named Larry, whom Stan kept referring to as "The Kid."

"The Kid", Todd had discovered, was actually a twenty-year-old man, newly returned from his sophomore year of college, working here at the Brewton Bar as a summer job. Even still, Stan seemed to prefer Todd's more seasoned countenance, and also seemed to miss what should have been obvious to a seasoned bartender's basic intuition: Todd desperately wanted to be alone.

Stan's death wouldn't be particularly gruesome. At least that was a gift. All Todd had seen was an elderly man in a recliner, oxygen tubing winding its way around his ears and into his nose. He could tell from the sounds in the vision that Stan was watching a game of baseball when he sagged down further into the comfort of his chair; a man at peace, going peacefully.

But this peaceful end-of-life scene was quite opposite of the one Todd was enduring at this very moment as Stan continued yapping in his car.

"So then I told her, 'Young lady, you live in my house. You've gotta abide by my rules,' but did she listen?" Stan paused long enough, Todd realized he was expecting an actual verbal response. Todd cleared his throat softly.

"I'm guessing she didn't."

"No, she didn't. And you know what she said?"

"What did she say?"

"She said, 'Fine Daddy, I'll just move in with Shawn instead.'"
Todd's blood turned cold.

"What did you just say?"

"I told her, 'HELL, NO!' Can you believe she'd rather live with a man she's been seeing for a handful of weeks than with her parents who have loved her all the days of her life?!" Todd glanced into the eyes of this man he hardly knew, but somehow felt connected to by the threads of shared fear. His voice had sounded angry, but his eyes were soft and sad. "But of course, she's nineteen. There's nothing I can really do to stop her."

"Have you...have you actually met this Shawn?"

"It's a small town, Todd, and I'm a bartender."

"I'll take that as a yes."

"Yeah, I've seen him. Though, I don't know what my baby girl sees in that man... Sometimes I think Margery was right, skipping town the night before her wedding. And it's damn creepy he seems to be moving on so quickly, like she meant nothing to him after all those years together. It ain't right."

"Margery?" Todd asked, feigning ignorance.

"Oh! Margery was his fiancée. They were engaged for something like two years before they finally set a date. Of course, they were living together and all, but then—the night before the wedding—*she disappeared*. At first, no one knew where she had gone, but then Helen told us all that the wedding was canceled. Rumor has it she'd run off with some truck driver and was headed north. NORTH! Can you believe it?"

"Wow," Todd said, pretending to be dumbstruck.

"She got cold feet. Or she got wise. Hard to tell which. But now that my Trisha's involved with the likes of Shawn... I don't know, I think I sorta wish she'd run off with a trucker too, if it meant keeping her away from the likes of him."

"What do you mean?"

Stan leaned in conspiratorially.

"You don't know? I guess you aren't from around here, are you? Well then, let me tell you what happened the day of the wedding."

MARGERY

ONCE THE INITIAL shock of her mother's hospital stay had settled a bit, and the chicken wings and blue cheese dressing had begun to do their work in calming her anxious nerves, Margery began to feel a strange itch, which she realized could only be the result of being home.

It was like putting on a sweater that had shrunk in the wash; every movement grated against her skin like she was wearing something tight and ill-fitting. Somehow she didn't belong in this life anymore. Even just the conversations with the kind, but curious nurses, who had known her family all her life, reminded her how the last time she was here, she had been about to get married. She couldn't help but notice when they turned toward each other and whispered when they thought she wasn't looking.

And then I...left? Was kidnapped? Kidnapped and then left to go further north of my own volition?

In the calming of her anger since their last conversation, Margery had been playing over all those little moments with Todd during their weeks together: the way he insisted she decide where they go next, the way he cared for her when she was brutally hungover and introduced her to Betsy and Mike, the beauty he'd shown her along their journey, and the goodness of his heart that was, despite his morally grey actions, the reason she was still alive.

"If I had to choose—your life, or your love—I'd choose your life every time. You are a star, Margery. The damn brightest light in the

dark I've ever seen. And the world is a much better place with you in it. Trust me. I've seen the alternative."

His last words to her played over and over in her mind. And every time she looked over at her mother, and saw the twinkling of mischief in her eyes, the realization hit her like a stone. *If Todd hadn't done what he did... I'd be dead and my mother would be sitting in this hospital bed alone.* But the weight of the lie still nagged at her, dragging down even their most joyful memories and covering them with a cloud of suspicion she wasn't sure how to clear.

One thing she did know for sure, was that now that she was back, the itchy and too-small sweater of her life in Brewton, Alabama, had to come off. She needed closure before she could figure out what was next.

IT WASN'T cancer.

Margery had called in another specialist to look at her mother's test results. And then another, just to be sure. The first doctor had his ass handed to him by both of the new doctors for needlessly freaking out Margery and Helen, and Margery wished she could see the look on Todd's face as she told him, *"You were right. She's going to be okay."*

Margery and her mother spent the week swapping stories. He mother recounted her most recent murder mysteries and contemporary romance novels she'd loved, and Margery told her all about their roadtrip adventures, described every delicious thing they had eaten or beautiful place they had seen, and Helen ate up every minute of it. They laughed until their sides ached, and Margery felt closer to her mother than she had in a long, long time. It was as though she could see it now, in even starker relief: Life was so very precious. More precious than most people truly imagined.

A week later, after all the lingering effects of Helen's fall

and subsequent head injury had mostly resolved, Margery took her mother home. When Helen had situated herself comfortably in her favorite wingback armchair in the living room and begun reading her new *Thursday Murder Club* novel, Margery backed slowly out of the room as though she were afraid of disturbing her mother's peace. But, of course, the peace she was truly about to disturb was her own.

"Shawn should be at the club right now. I overheard one of the nurses saying he's been playing every Tuesday at four, with her son, Jimmy." Margery turned toward her mother's smiling face as Helen glanced at her over her readers.

"How did you know where I was going?" Her mother laid her still-open book gently in her lap, her worn thumb marking her place.

"You've been…on a journey Margery, dear. And now you've come back. But it's time to get your things from that low-life's overpriced suburban nightmare, and move on with your life. *Your own life.* Your real life, baby." Her words rang with a truth and tenderness that made Margery's throat tighten.

"I feel like I'm starting completely over." Her mother's eyes sparkled with joy and also with a whisper of tears.

"I know, baby. And that may be so, but I've always found the most painful endings are just the compost for beautiful new beginnings." Margery smiled at her then. The afternoon sunshine was playing in her mother's grey hair where she'd twisted it up with a claw clip. At once, she looked angelic, and somehow, even more firmly and beautifully earthly. Earthly, like wildflowers, or blueberries, or the color of the sky as you can only see it from the ground.

Margery took a deep breath of this reassurance that her mother was fully alive, here and now before she said, "Thanks, Mom." Then, she grabbed her keys from the hook on the wall and walked out the front door, closing it firmly behind her.

Margery hadn't been sure what to expect; but this hadn't been it. After driving around in her small sedan for a few extra blocks to make sure Shawn was well and truly gone, she'd gone to the front door and put her key in the lock.

It didn't work.

That's strange.

Then she'd gone to the mailbox and checked to see if there was anything for her. What she saw chilled her. Where their two names had once sat side-by-cohabitating-side, she saw only 'SHAWN PENNINGTON' and a jagged scribble of sharpie blacking out where her name had once been.

I suppose I deserve that.

That was when she looked up from her place at the curb and saw the red dumpster peeking around the corner of the garage.

That's new. Is he remodeling or something?

She walked over, curious. But when she looked inside, her heart sank into her feet.

It was full of her things: her soft cotton dresses, her favorite pair of jeans, the painting she'd bought at last year's art market, and worst of all... her books. She leaned over the side of the dumpster to try and reach the volumes, but she pretty quickly realized she was going to have to climb in if she wanted to get all of her things out.

She was still staring at all her worldly possessions, which had been tossed into the dumpster like garbage by the man she'd once shared a life with, when she heard a car door slam and the sound of eerily familiar footsteps behind her.

"Hey, baby," Shawn crooned, his voice grating over her skin, leaving gooseflesh in its wake. "You're home."

TODD

Todd leaned his head against the wheel of his truck as he stared at the text thread with Margery. He'd been contemplating sending her a message every single day for the last week, but he kept coming up empty, having no idea how to start a conversation with her now. Betsy's words from a few days earlier played over and over again in his mind.

"Chin up, Todd. She told you to go, and she very well may ask you to come back, but you need to give it time. You told her the truth and now... now it's up to her. You didn't give her a choice to go with you that first time, so you'll have to give her the choice now."

Todd leaned back in his seat and sighed. He typed. Sighed again. And put his phone away without pressing send.

TODD: I miss you.

MARGERY

Margery froze at the sound of Shawn's voice and the barely restrained violence in it. She turned slowly toward him and lifted her chin.

"It's hardly my home when my key won't even go in the lock. Besides, you never deigned to add me to the title anyway." *Even if I was paying half the bills.*

Shawn snorted.

"And a good thing too. Or else this whole 'break up' would have gotten a whole lot…messier." His eyes were gleaming in a way that scared her. "That is what this is, right, baby? You leave me at the altar and then sneak back here weeks

later to try and get your stuff when you think I'll be gone?"
He set down his golf bag and picked up a driver, swinging it
experimentally in a way Margery knew was far from casual.

"I'm sorry it took me so long to end things, Shawn.
That... that wasn't fair to you." Shawn gave a bitter laugh and
lurched towards her.

"Fair!? Fair would have been you marrying me like you
promised when I gave you this!" He threw down the club and
snatched her left hand, lifting it as if to show her the ring.
The ring she was not wearing.

"I took it off a few weeks ago," she said, pulling a small
box out of her pocket and holding it out to him. "After I
called off the wedding. Here."

Shawn snatched the box and tossed it into his golf bag.
"I suppose you expect me to thank you for giving it back."

"I... I don't expect anything Shawn... I just came..."

"To get your stuff back. Yeah, I gathered that. How long
have you been in town anyway, Margery? I heard you've been
at the hospital for a week. A WEEK. And you couldn't spare
a single moment to call? Text? Let me know you're back in
town?" His smile was the saccharine thing she'd once considered charming.

"I..." Margery stammered, "I wasn't ready."

"And I suppose that's why you called off the wedding, too
isn't it? You weren't 'ready'. After you'd been bitching at me
for years to propose, and then for the years of our engage-
ment to pick a fucking date, when it all came down to it, you
still weren't 'ready' were you?"

"That's not why I left!" She felt her voice rising an octave
and shivered at the look of contempt solidifying his features.
"Why is all my stuff in this dumpster?"

"I was tired of holding on to your shit."

"Shawn, it's been three weeks. And you could have asked
my mother to..."

"Feels a lot longer for those of us not gallivanting around

the country with a fucking trucker." Margery's face burned bright red. "So, the rumors are true. You've met someone else, is that it? Some other dick tickles your fancy like I can't? Is that it? I bet you just wanted to know how the blue-collar crowd does it." His smile was dripping with violence as he towered over her. She put out a hand and held it toward him, palm up. Her fingertips were only an inch from his chest.

"Back up, Shawn."

"What? I can't even stand near my own fiancée anymore? Not even after she ditched me on our wedding day?" He took another step closer, the front of his golf shirt and his hard chest pressing into her hand, making her elbow bend slightly.

"I'm not your fiancée anymore, and I said BACK. UP." Margery glared into his face, trying to match his menace and swagger, but behind her back she slipped her phone out of her pocket and sent a text. A few moments later, her heart lifted as she felt the small vibration in her pocket—a sign her message had been received.

TODD

MARGERY: NEED YOU

TODD WAS driving like a bat out of hell.
Flying like a bat out of hell?
Driving like a trucker who'd just gotten this startling text from the woman he loved, but hadn't spoken to in a week after his big revelation.

TODD: ON MY WAY. JUST KEEP YOUR LOCATION SHARING ON.

Thank God he'd kept taking small contract carrier jobs in the Alabama, Mississippi, Georgia, and Tennessee area. Thank God, that though he'd gone to stay with Betsy and Mike for a day earlier in the week, he hadn't gone much farther.

Something—that niggling premonition he couldn't quite shake—had told him to stay close. And by Margery's second message, he knew that, *something*, had been right.

MARGERY: SHAWN HERE

Todd drove even faster.

MARGERY

THIS STANDOFF WITH Shawn had been going on for the better part of thirty minutes. She wasn't sure how much longer it would take for the storm of Shawn's rage to blow out, or if it even would, before he'd broken something far beyond repair.

"I'm just here for some closure, Shawn. So we can both move on with our lives."

"You think you're better than me, don't you? You think you can just go off and 'move on' and have your little adventures and leave me behind without consequences? You only care about this stuff I've thrown out, when it was US, *you* threw in the garbage." Shawn was stalking around the dumpster now, flipping the two-part lid open with a flick of his hand and peering in to examine the contents. "You know, the trash guys are supposed to come get this later this week. But I don't see a reason to wait, do you? After all, you've already thrown a match on everything else of value." He strode

over to the now open garage door and grabbed the small gas can from where he'd stashed it next to the lawnmower. "What do you say we just go ahead and get that last measure of 'closure' right now. There's a lot of paper in there you know. I didn't know you had so many books until I nearly broke my back dumping them all in there."

"No! Please, Shawn, that's not necessary. I'll just take my stuff and…"

"And what!? Leave? Again? I'm not going to make it that easy for you this time Margery." He lifted the gas can over his head and began to tip it toward the open dumpster.

"NO!" Margery yelled, trying to hold back the tears threatening to well in her eyes. *They're just books,* she told herself, *they're not worth your life.*

The sound of an engine roared up the street and pulled to a screaming stop behind her, at the foot of the driveway. *I'd know that engine anywhere.*

She watched as Shawn's eyes lifted, at first in surprise, and then reverted to rage, but before he could get another word out, she heard the truck door open and another voice come booming across the pavement.

"Hey, asshole! Don't you know you need a permit for a dumpster fire that big?"

Margery turned toward Todd as relief flooded her. He leapt from the cab and walked toward her with that self-assured smirk plastered to his face. His chin dimple was doing its dimply things, and her heart… her heart was singing a song that sounded something like: *He came. He's here. He came. He's here.*

CHAPTER NINE
Comeuppance & a Blueberry Festival

TODD

IT TOOK EVERYTHING Todd had in him to keep his strides measured instead of rushing at the asshole that had Margery and her belongings at his mercy. *Or lack of mercy as the case may be.* But he knew Shawn loved nothing more than a power trip, and staying calm would give him the upper hand. *At least for now.*

He kept his temper tightly coiled as he sauntered over to where Margery stood by the red dumpster, which he guessed might be full of her belongings; belongings Shawn was currently threatening to destroy with a gas can and a match. He swept a glance from her sandals to her hair, noticing that her face was red and her chest splotchy, most likely due to her confrontation with Shawn, but otherwise she seemed to be unharmed.

"Are you okay?" he asked softly, and Margery turned to

him with wide, grateful eyes. There was something in their depths that he couldn't quite place, but it was a warmth he knew must also be shining out of his own features. After weeks on the road with her, he'd grown accustomed to her presence, and fuck, he'd missed her. He couldn't think of the last time he'd allowed himself to get close enough to someone that he actually *missed* them when they weren't around. Margery nodded slightly, confirming she was unharmed. But Todd wasn't sure how much longer that would be true for her belongings. He took stock of the situation, glancing between Margery, the dumpster, the oversized ranch house in front of him, and the other man—if you could call him that.

Shawn was tall, standing well over six feet, with the lean muscle of a man who had plenty of time to kill working out at the country club gym. His hair was clipped short, the front of it gelled in an attempt at a style that seemed to have failed to do anything more than make him look like an overgrown child with a cowlick. His green golf shirt and khaki pants, confirmed Todd's suspicions.

Yup. He's a complete and total tool.

Though Shawn had frozen when Todd first arrived, the gas can still suspended over the dumpster's contents, there seemed to be a war in his eyes about what to do next. Shawn scowled, as though he were sizing up what kind of threat Todd might pose now that he'd arrived on the scene.

"I suggest you put the gas can down, Shawn."

"It's you," Shawn hissed.

"Me?" Todd smiled with mock innocence.

"The asshole who stole my bride the night before our wedding."

"Oh! Yeah. That's me." Todd smiled again, showing all his teeth, then took a step closer to Margery. Shawn looked between them, his face purpling with rage.

"You think you can just take her from me? SHE'S MINE."

"Actually," Todd began softly, but there was a bite to each and every one of his words, "Margery is a free person who belongs only, and always, to herself. I just wanted to give her a chance to live long enough so she could find that out for herself." He looked at Margery then and smiled tenderly, affection gleaming in his eyes. Margery returned a small smile before dipping her head in embarrassment. "And as a free person, she should be free to retrieve her belongings from her previous residence without their destruction by assholes that don't even understand fire codes."

Shawn only hoisted the gas can higher, causing a splash of gasoline to pour onto some unknown object in the dumpster.

"NO! Please, Shawn, don't!" Margery screamed, tears beginning to gather in her eyes. Shawn held her gaze without the slightest hint of compassion or pity. His eyes were full of violence and Todd knew Margery's belongings were not the only thing he longed to destroy.

If Todd was going to be able to save Margery's belongings, he'd have to choose his next words very, very carefully.

"So you'd rather spend your time lighting a literal dumpster fire than facing up to the man who stole 'your bride' away the night before your wedding?" Todd goaded, moving away from Margery and toward the bag of golf clubs discarded in the grass on the opposite side of the driveway. Shawn's face snapped toward him. *Good.*

"You're right," Shawn said finally, "first things first." He dropped the gas can to the driveway and didn't notice when it fell on its side and gas began slowly leaking out and down the driveway. He picked up the driver where he'd left it by the dumpster, and when he turned again to face Todd, they were both holding golf clubs. "I'll have plenty of time to make Margery regret all her very poor decisions, after I've dealt with *you*." He held the club in two hands and swung it back and forth experimentally. "I hope you're ready to die,

Trucker Boy."

"The name's Todd. And I've lived my whole life in the shadow of death, Shawn," Todd said easily, "but I don't think you'll be the one to send me to glory. Not yet, anyway." He briefly flicked his eyes toward Margery and winked. Her lips turned upward in the tiniest hint of a smile.

"Yeah, man, whatever. I'm still gonna kick your ass." Without another warning, Shawn ran toward Todd and swung the golf club directly at his head, but Todd's reaction was fast and he easily ducked out of the way. Shawn came at him again, this time holding the club over his head like he was preparing to split a chunk of wood, and once again, Todd spun out of the way, just as the club came down.

"I really ought to tell you," Todd said, "that when I was a teenager, I used to play fight with lightsabers every day with my neighbor." Shawn's face was red with rage and he let out a vicious laugh.

"STUPID FUCKING NERD! I don't know what on *earth* Margery sees in you!" Todd blocked another blow with his club, then advanced, swinging low and catching Shawn in the ankles before Shawn could react. Shawn went sprawling, his club clattering to the ground as his body landed on the pavement with a thud. Todd stood over him, the club Shawn had been wielding pinned underneath Todd's boot.

"What I was trying to tell you, young Padawan, is that *I'm very, very good at pretend sword fighting.*" Shawn's eyes were burning coals of defiance at his own defeat, as the sound of sirens rounded the corner in the neighborhood. He tried to dislodge the club from beneath Todd's boot, but he couldn't get any leverage wile laid out prone on the driveway like the piece of garbage he was.

Todd tossed his own club into the grass as the cops pulled up, and leaning toward Shawn, he said in a low voice, "I think that's your ride."

SHAWN WAS charged with attempted assault and destruction of property. Though only a small amount of gasoline had actually landed on any of Margery's belongings, those items were thoroughly ruined. With Margery's testimony, her admittance of all the fear and abuse she'd suffered during those long years she and Shawn had been together, and a promise by her and Todd to come forward as witnesses, and testify to Shawn's violent and disturbing behavior, the Sheriff was confident he'd get some court-ordered anger management, along with some potential jail time. Even still, the only thing Todd could think was: *It's not enough. It never is.* The Sheriff was taking the final notes for Margery's statement while Todd casually strolled over to the back of the cop car where Shawn sat, with his hands cuffed behind his back, his face fuming.

"This is all your fault you worthless piece of—"

"If you don't mind," Todd hissed, "I think I'll do the talking for a while." Shawn glared into Todd's face, but something about Todd's tone of voice made him shut up and listen. "I have a secret Shawn. A very, *very* big secret." Sean's eyes widened slightly. "A secret you could probably try and use against me, if you ever wanted to. Would you like to know what it is?"

"Why wouldn't I? I owe you big for what you did to me. And I ain't through with trying to get my justice."

"I know, Shawn." Todd said, almost sadly, "I know you're not. The second you get let out on bail, you'll come straight for Margery again. And that's the problem." Shawn stared blankly, trying to track with what Todd was saying. "I have... *a gift,* Shawn. When I look into someone's eyes for the first time—the way I did with you just a bit ago, before you went all caveman and tried to club me to death with your sporting equipment—I can see the moment they are going to die." He looked meaningfully at Shawn as the disbelief, and then

the horror, began to wash over his face.

"You're...you're crazy! You're delusional! They should have you locked up! You should be—you should be— "

"Probably, yes. Perhaps all that is true, Shawn. But that's not what I wanted to tell you. What I wanted to tell you, *is how you die, Shawn.* Because you are going to die one day, you know. None of us gets to go on living forever." Shawn's face blanched, his mouth working, but no words came out. "Now, mind you, Shawn, this isn't a future set in stone. I've learned that much over the past month. This is only the path you are on right now. But boy, is it a bleak one. If I were you Shawn..." He scrubbed a hand over his forehead in mock sympathy. "If I were you, I'd try to get on a different one." All the rage seemed to leach from Shawn in a moment, leaving behind only a pale-faced terror.

"What... What did you see?" Shawn said in almost a whisper. The control had been sapped from him. His confidence had guttered. And now he was at Todd's mercy, begging for a knowledge Todd knew would haunt him until Shawn took his final breath.

"Isn't it obvious? You die here. In that house, right there, surrounded by PBR beer cans, the TV blaring *I love Lucy* reruns. I saw a side table full of picture frames, but do you know who was in them?"

"Who?" Shawn whisper-shouted. "Who was in the frames?" His eyes were wide with terror and he seemed like he was nearly hyperventilating.

"No one, Shawn. They were all empty frames with the photos torn out, only the cardboard backing remaining. There were photos of you with someone else's face cut out of the shot, or in some cases scribbled over. But most of the photos were of those cheesy models who come with the frame. And do you know what that tells me? It tells me you die alone, Shawn. And no one mourns you. Because you single-handedly destroyed every good thing you ever had in

your life. Just like you almost destroyed her."

MARGERY

MARGERY COULDN'T hear what Todd was saying to Shawn as he leaned a hip on the Sheriff's vehicle parked right behind Shawn's red Camero, but she watched as Shawn went from flushed with anger, to a ghostly pale shade she'd never seen on him before. She'd seen her own pale face in the mirror more times than she could count; her neck lined with fingerprint bruises, her eyes shadowed like she'd been planning a run on the high-fashion circuit.
After a few more minutes, Todd tipped his head toward Shawn in mock salute and walked back toward her.

"If you think of anything else, please don't hesitate to give us a call, Miss Daniels."

"I will. Thank you, Jeff," she said softly.

"Shall we?" Todd said, extending his arm to Margery. "What do you say we come back and get all your stuff tomorrow? I can pick up a small trailer and we'll get it all taken care of for you. I've already asked your mom if she can send one of her friends over to grab your car. It's been... a lot of excitement for one day." He looked at her meaningfully, his mouth smiling, but his eyes were tinged with worry and concern. She smiled back, in gratitude.

"Yeah, that sounds great. Thank you." She was rewarded by his smile actually reaching the corners of his eyes.

"Are you hungry?"

"Starved."

"I hear there's a blueberry festival going on..." Todd said, his eyebrows lifting in question. "Would you care to accompany me?"

"You read my mind, Todd Mackewain."

"Is what I'm wearing okay?" he asked. "This is your hometown, after all. I don't want to embarrass you."

"You love to embarrass me."

"Only in a good way," he said, smiling.

"You look..." She took a moment to take him in. His dark hair looked like he'd been running his hands through it, and he was sporting his trademark, two-day stubble. He was wearing a clean pair of jeans and what she'd come to know was his favorite T-shirt. But the most incredible part of his ensemble was, without a doubt, those sparkling gray eyes, and the gentle smile that she knew was not at all part of the charming facade he so often affected with others, but the gentle, honest, open smile he shared only with those he truly loved. "You look perfect," she said at last, her face coloring.

But she didn't look away. And neither did he. And a comfortable understanding passed between them, as if in the meeting of their eyes they had already said all that needed to be said.

TODD DROVE them out of the suburbs and into the center of town where the Alabama Blueberry Festival was well underway at Jennings Park in the heart of Brewton. The park was a beautiful open green field, fenced in by a lush canopy of trees which shaded an array of picnic tables where couples, friends, and families had already begun to stake out their own patches of shade. It was a warm June day and the air was humid, but the heat was not overbearing and there was a delightful breeze that danced its way across Margery's skin, cooling her with its gentle caress.

Every year since Margery had been a little girl, she'd looked forward to the annual tradition of the park being transformed into a feast for the eyes and the stomach. Craft vendors, boutique shops, and vintage finds were scattered throughout the tents, along with blueberry delicacies of

every variety. Cobblers, pies, wines, and popsicles mingled with the more savory fare of fried chicken and waffles with blueberry compote, blueberry cornbread muffins, and turkey cheese sandwiches with a thyme and blueberry Jam.

They had parked Todd's truck off one of the many side streets, and were joining the throng entering the park just in time for the dinner hour when Margery finally broke the silence between them.

"My mother used to take off every blueberry festival day."

"Oh?"

"Mmmhmmm. It was one of the few local holidays we enjoyed together every year, no matter what."

"I can see why," Todd said glancing around at the tents, the food trucks, and the crowd gathered from far and wide to celebrate the simple joy of a summer fruit.

"It's some of the best food of the year," she said. "So I figured it'd be right up your alley." She looped an arm through his.

"You know me so well," he said smiling down at her in a way that was somehow teasing, and also tender. She fought down a blush.

They wove between the wide array of booths, food trucks, and screaming children for thirty minutes before finally settling on the vendor with the turkey, brie and blueberry jam sandwiches. The deciding factor had, of course, been the fact that Todd discovered the sandwich maker made his sourdough bread from scratch, along with the line being quite a bit longer than the line at the chicken and waffles place.

"A long line is always a good sign when it comes to food," Todd said as they joined the queue.

"Yes, yes," Margery replied, "I've heard this speech before."

Todd cleared his throat. "About... about before," he said, releasing her arm to turn toward her, all signs of teasing

gone. "I really am sorry I lied to you... I just...", He paused, seemingly at a loss for words, and ran his hand through his hair.

"You saved my life, Todd… you took a risk, went against everything you thought you knew about your gift because you couldn't stand idly by and let me marry that...," She swallowed hard. "Well... you met him." She flicked her eyes up to his and something like shame washed over her.

"Yeah," he said, "I did."

"I think I was just afraid that everything we shared... those three weeks on the road together... I was afraid maybe none of it was real."

Todd looked at Margery, startled, and his eyes held the depths of his surprise as he turned toward her more fully.

"Margery... of all the probabilities and possibilities in this world—the ones I'm the MOST grateful for—were the ones that led me to meeting you."

Her heart leapt into her throat at his words, and she felt the tears rising in her eyes as she stared at him. He stared back at her, his eyes shining.

"I'm..." she said, almost in a whisper, "I'm so glad I met you, too.

Just then, another couple walked up behind them in line and started talking in animated voices. "And then, one of the officers lit up just before they were headed back to the station, you know how old Stoneface smokes like a chimney, but he didn't notice there was gas spilling from a can up by the dumpster, and I guess a puddle must have formed beneath that shiny red Camaro or something, because Trisha said when she got there to pick it up for the car show, *it was on FIRE!*"

Todd was still staring at Margery, but his gaze had shifted from the softness of tender feelings, to surprise, and finally, to a look of mock horror as they listened to the couple behind them. He pressed his lips together firmly to

stifle a laugh, and Margery felt herself attempting to do the same. Todd turned back to examine the menu of the food truck even though he'd long ago decided exactly what he was going to order.

"Boy, oh boy, I'm hungry. How about you?" he said finally, trying to change the subject.

She couldn't hold it in another moment. Todd's sudden attempt at casual speech had broken the very last levy in Margery's restraint, and she began laughing.

It was her real laugh. Not the polite version she'd been trained to give for company. Not the fake, feminine laugh she'd perfected during those years of forcing herself to laugh at Shawn's mediocre jokes. This was an obscene, cackling sound that broke free from her chest like a spirit released from the depths of Hell. Her face turned red, her shoulders shook, and she worried she might pass out if she didn't start breathing again soon, but still she laughed.

"Margery? Marge, are you okay?" Todd asked, turning back to her and running a hand back and forth across her shoulder blades, then patting her gently, as though that motion might exorcise the giggling demon.

"It's the final revenge!" she shrieked breathlessly. Her laughter nearly sounded like sobbing, and there were fat tears sliding down her face as her shoulders continued to shake. "He. Loved. That. Car. More. Than. ME!" After a few more moments of manic laughter, she saw they were getting closer to the front of the line, so she tried to take some deep, controlled breaths to calm herself.

"Then he's an even bigger idiot than I thought," Todd said, smiling at her, wiping her tears from her face with his thumb. His calloused fingers on her skin sparked a different sort of joy within her that felt familiar and safe, but one that she wasn't ready to name.

A few minutes later, the laughter finally subsiding, and warm, savory, sweet sandwiches in hand, Margery and

Todd walked to the edge of the park and sat in the shade of a sycamore tree.

"Can I ask you something?" Margery began after she'd taken a few large bites.

"Of course."

"How did you get to Shawn's so quickly today?"
Todd took a bite of his sandwich and chewed thoughtfully.

"I had a feeling... sometimes I get these feelings, you know. I decided to stay close. The farthest I went recently was Betsy and Mike's. I just took small contracts within a few hours of here. When your message came in, I was in Castlewood dropping off a trailer."

"Oh," Margery said, taking another bite of her sandwich.

"Can I ask *you* something?" Todd said, shifting his shoulder into hers where they sat side by side at the picnic table.

"Of course."

"Why did you text me?"

Margery flushed. "Because... " she said, almost defensively, "because you are the only man I really know I can trust."
The words felt shallow and small—like they would never be enough to tell him what she desperately wanted him to know. That even though he'd lied to her, and their roadtrip had begun with what was *technically* a kidnapping, he was the only man in her life that had ever made her feel safe... *loved.*

"It was an...interesting choice of words," he said, smiling at her mischievously.

"Oh, I just sent you what I already had typed out." She felt her face drain of color as she realized what she'd just revealed. Todd gave her his trademark smirk and she knew he'd never let it go.

"'Need you'. That was the message you had cued up to send?" Margery felt her face go from white, to pink, to red.

"So what! You need me too!" She tried to glare, but had

the feeling she was failing as she stared into his eyes. She took another bite and chewed slowly, then she cleared her throat. "After all, without me, you'd just be the harbinger of death, running around the country with shipments of maple syrup."

Todd watched her thoughtfully, but said nothing, taking another bite of his sandwich instead. Margery followed suit.

"Oh my God, this is so good. Is there a job where I can just eat delicious things all day?" She licked a drop of blueberry jam from her lower lip, and noticed Todd tracking the movement. The tension that had been coiled between them all these weeks suddenly pulled as taut as a bow string.

"Oh my God, are you going to kiss me?" she asked, something like a mixture of nerves and delight snaking its way up her spine.

Todd let out a laugh. "I was… considering it." He licked his lips and gave her a wicked grin. "Would that be okay? If I kissed you?" He was teasing her again and she felt herself blushing… again.

"You know, eventually this game of, 'How red can I get Margery to blush?' isn't going to be fun anymore, and then you're going to have to find someone else to play with." She turned back to her sandwich and prepared to take another giant bite.

"Hmm," he said, snatching the bread from her hands and setting it back in the to-go container beside her. "I don't think you're right about that one, Margery…and besides…you didn't answer my question." He licked a drop of blueberry jam from his thumb and stared at her with such an intoxicating mix of amusement and longing that Margery could scarcely breathe.

"Yes," she heard herself say, but she was frozen to the spot. Her heart was hammering in her chest so hard she wondered if he could hear it. "Yes, it would be okay if you kissed me."

Then Todd threaded his fingers through the hair at the base of her neck, and gently pulled her closer. Then his lips were on hers.

The kiss was gentle and sweet, and Todd tasted like blueberries and brie and sourdough bread, and Margery knew for sure, that though her life had been saved in one way, it had been ruined, too.

"I'll never love anyone else the way I love him," she thought almost absently, as though thinking the words could stop her from falling headfirst for this supernatural trucker named Todd Mackewain; a man from everywhere and nowhere. She wasn't sure about all the probabilities of possibilities the future held for her now, but she felt certain she'd want him in every version of the future she'd now live to see because of him.

After a moment, Todd pulled back, as though he could sense the chaotic swirling of her thoughts at that very moment. Resting his head against hers, he whispered, "For the record, I don't think I'll ever, *ever*, get tired of playing with you."

CHAPTER TEN
Love's Fulfillment & a New Adventure

MARGERY

THEY STAYED until the fireflies came out and the bonfire raged. All night long, Todd had strayed no more than an arm's length away from her, and she realized, though he'd played it cool with Shawn, he was far from unaffected by the danger she'd faced.

"You wanna call it a night?" Todd asked, almost too casually, as he draped his arm across her shoulders. Firelight danced across the planes of his face as Margery considered him. He turned his face slightly in her direction, the left corner of his mouth quirking up in that sweet and mischievous way of his, yet his eyes were soft and seeking, asking her what she wanted.

"Actually," she said softly, "I was just thinking, earlier tonight, about how much I miss my bed in your truck." It might not have been exactly true, but it was close enough to the truth for the moment. *The mattress wasn't THAT bad.*

"*Your*, bed eh?" His smile widened and Margery's face

burned.

"You know what I mean! The bunk I always slept in. You know, after you *kidnapped* me?" She elbowed him sharply in the ribs and Todd didn't even try to dodge her attack.

"Alright, alright, I deserved that," he said, laughing softly. "You ready to go, then?" She looked around at the crowd. Some of them were out-of-towners. Some of them, people whom she'd known her entire life. And yet, the man standing next to her was the only one here who really *saw* her.

She leaned into him then, and threading her fingers through Todd's larger ones, she said with a confidence she hadn't known she possessed, "Take me home Todd."

T HEY WALKED OUT of the park and into the dimly lit streets. All the shops had been closed early tonight for the festival, and what was often a lively street, felt suddenly desolate and abandoned. Margery shivered.

"You cold?" Todd asked, pulling her in closer and chafing her arm.

"I'm alright," she said, her face coloring slightly. Somehow, even in the dark, Todd seemed to be able to sense her flush and know exactly what it was about.

"Nothing has to happen, you know Margery...even if you want to just hang out and watch an old Friends episode—" She pressed a finger to his lips to stop him from speaking.

"What if I want something to happen?"

She could feel his smile spreading beneath her fingertips, though her eyes were still adjusting to the dark and she couldn't see it. She moved her hand to the side of his face and stroked a thumb across his rough cheek. He reached up and trapped her hand there, turning his lips against her palm, kissing it gently. His lips then moved across the plane of her hand, trailing light kisses across each and every fingertip.

"Then I'd be honored to oblige," he said, eyes locking with hers. He looked at her as though she were the light he couldn't stop seeing, despite all that life had thrown at him.

They walked toward the side street where Todd had parked, and Margery was surprised when Todd hopped into the driver's seat. "As much as I'd love to ravish you right here in the middle of your charming town, I hear the thing about small towns is that...people talk," he said, grinning devilishly in a way that made Margery's toes curl.

They didn't drive far; just far enough outside of town they could find a convenient truck stop with all the necessary things they'd need in the morning. They'd stayed at places like this, dozens of times before, over their weeks of traveling together, but Margery's stomach had never been somersaulting the way it was now. She was pretty sure she was still red from when Todd had kissed her hand in the street. Todd parked, and then his gaze turned toward her. He looked at her like a man who was starving—like a man who hadn't let himself take a long look in all this time, and now, he finally dared.

"So..." Margery said, her gaze sliding over to him. She let herself inhale his scent; the woodsy musk, the scent of rain. She took in the way his T-shirt hugged his broad shoulders.

"So..." he said, and reached a hand out toward her, and together they stood and made their way toward the back of the cab. She knew, at every moment, the choice was hers. She felt so incredibly safe with this man, and she knew that whatever happened tonight, come morning, he'd still be there, smiling at her with that infernal grin, teasing her and taunting her and making her laugh at herself. He'd be there, feeding her with the most delicious, hole-in-the-wall food that money could buy. He'd be there making sure she chose not him—but herself. Again, and again. She turned toward him and nestled her hand in his and stood.

With the engine power shut off, only the battery-powered running lights were illuminating the warm summer darkness, and the light reflected softly in Todd's eyes. He took a hand and stroked her cheek, brushing the curls back from her face and tucking them behind her ear.

"May I kiss you?" he breathed; not cautious, but reverent, somehow.

"Yes," she said, and leaned in to his solid warmth.

He brought his lips to hers, and it was not at all like the tender kiss they'd shared earlier in the park. Both of his hands were in her hair, tipping her face up to his. His tongue swept across the bottom edge of her lower lip until a small sound escaped her and her lips parted. Then his tongue swept into her mouth, and Margery had never known such pleasure. Somehow, this kiss made her feel as though she'd never truly been kissed before.

Todd tasted like a summer rain; like thirst, and the drink to quench it. His tongue danced with hers; advancing and retreating—pursuing her, and letting her pursue him. There was no overly masculine dominance in his kiss—only a gentle, persistent desire to *know her*. When they were both panting, Todd pulled back for a moment.

"May I..." he gestured to her clothing, specifically, the buttons on her cotton dress. She nodded furiously.

"Yes," she said, wanting him more than she'd ever wanted anything else. Her thighs clenched with anticipation and longing.

Todd's hands slipped down to the straps at her shoulders, his rough callouses bringing goosebumps to the surface of her skin wherever they touched. He slipped one strap off, then the other. Then he slowly undid the first few buttons at the front of her dres. Margery had the presence of mind to remember she wasn't wearing a bra, and there was very little standing between Todd and her bare breasts. The bodice undone, the fabric slid down to her hips of its own accord, and Todd took the opportunity to take her in. His rough hands traced the outer curves of her breasts before gently sliding beneath them. He bowed his head, lifting one gently to his lips, then the other. He kissed the spot just above the peaked nipple on each breast, and before she realized what she was doing, she grabbed his hips in her hands and pulled him into her. She felt the evidence of his desire for her pressing against her core and she whimpered into his hair.

"Todd...."she said, shifting her stance in impatience.

"Hmmmm?" he said, refusing to relinquish her nipple in order to speak.

"Should we..." She waved her hand vaguely in the direction of the bunk.

"Impatient, are we?" he said, lifting his head enough to kiss his way from her tormented nipples all the way up to her neck, where he began kissing and nipping the skin there until she was squirming.

"TODD!" she said.

"Yes, gorgeous?" The sounds he was wringing from her were making him cocky.

"I...I...I...."

"You, what, love?" He moved his mouth to the spot beneath her ear and sucked lightly, meanwhile his fingertips gently teased her nipples.

"I....want...you..." she said, her voice coming out breathy and hoarse.

"You've got me, gorgeous," he rasped out between kisses. "And I've got you. I'm going to get you there, okay? Trust me." He gave her another languid kiss on the mouth and when he released her, she found herself nodding furiously.

"I trust you, Todd." As though that statement was the cue he was waiting for, he shimmied her dress the rest of the way down her body, slid his hands behind her thighs, scooped her up in his arms, and pivoted them toward the lower bunk that had been Margery's all those weeks. The silk pillowcase Todd had bought her so she didn't constantly complain of "road hair" was still on the pillow, and Margery recognized the extra blanket she'd purchased from a gift shop in Idaho. But these were all the observations she could make before Todd's lips were on hers again, and the delicious weight of his body pressed between her thighs.

"Pants!" she rasped out between kisses.

"What about them?" he teased, pressing the hardness of his longing against the thin cotton of her underwear.

"OFF!" She felt like she was shouting, but desperately hoped that wasn't the case.

"Yes, ma'am," he said, smiling at her in the dark, and the

warmth of his body momentarily slipped away.

"Shirt—while you're at it," she whispered, stretching herself out on the mattress and curling her toes until they cracked deliciously.

When Todd returned, the smoothness of his skin warred with the sweetness of his lips for her attention. She smoothed her hands over his broad chest, memorizing his form. The thin cotton of his boxers, and the thin cotton of her panties was all that separated them now, and she felt the heady rush of his skin on her skin as he brought his chest flush with hers. He kept his arms braced on either side of her, as though he feared she was terribly fragile and might snap at any moment. She used an elbow and knocked one of his arms out from beneath him so he was forced to lean on her more.

"What are you..."

"I want to feel you," she said. "You aren't going to hurt me Todd." Even in the dark, she could feel the tenderness of his gaze and the kindness in his eyes. Almost at once his gaze turned from soft to mischievous.

"Like...this?" he asked, pressing into that aching spot between her thighs.

"Mmmmm....yeah," she said, almost gasping.

"And how about *this*..." he said, lifting himself slightly and rubbing his length against her with a roll of his hips.

She inhaled a gasp, but was otherwise struck nearly speechless so she just nodded.

"You are an impatient little thing aren't you?" Todd crooned, kissing his way from her mouth, to her earlobe, and continuing down her neck. Margery was a puddle with scarcely a thought in her head. Her skin flamed red with heat, but for once she didn't care. And Todd was still kissing his way down her body until he got to the edge of her underwear.

"Where are you going?" she asked, propping herself up on her elbows so she could see what he was doing.

"I'm not going anywhere, gorgeous. Just relax." She looked at him skeptically as he ran his thumb along the edge

of her underwear. "May I... kiss you?" he asked, his eyebrows raised in question. For a moment Margery didn't understand what he meant, and then... *Ohhh...OHHHHH!*

"Are you...are you sure? You don't have to do that..." she stammered.

"I'm not offering to do anything I don't wholeheartedly want to do, Margery," Todd said, suddenly serious. "And you shouldn't either." She almost felt self-conscious in this moment, but with the look on Todd's face, the feeling floated away. She nodded her consent, and Todd made quick work of her underwear, sliding them down her legs and tossing them in the corner of the sleeper cab with the rest of their clothes. Then Todd's broad hands were on the insides of her knees, gently pressing them open. When she relaxed her legs at his gentle prompting, he began sliding his hands up her thighs so painfully slowly, Margery thought she might explode. *Or, implode. Whichever.*

Todd brought his thumb to the apex of her thighs, gently circling her sensitive bundle of nerves, before dipping down to her molten center and swearing at the wetness he found there.

"Damn, Margery, you're so fucking sexy," he said, bracing his hands on the insides of her thighs and lowering his face to her. He looked up at her from beneath his eyelashes and smiled slightly to see that she was still watching him on propped up elbows. Then she felt his tongue sweep from her entrance to the top of her clit in one smooth stroke that had her elbows collapsing.

"*I never knew it could be this good,*" she thought to herself, as Todd tormented her with intense, teasing strokes, as the pleasure ratcheted up her spine and curled like a tidal wave about to crash back down in her lower belly. Her hips began to buck of their own volition, but Todd placed a firm hand on them,keeping her still, allowing her to take only what he would give.

And he *gave.*

Before long, Margery was panting and gasping. The pressure was building to a fever pitch, and she wondered if

there was an edge to this waterfall she felt herself careening towards. Her hands were fisting in the silk of her pillowcase as she finally fell off the edge.

She was pretty sure breathing deeply was still import-ant, but she couldn't quite do more than take the shallowest breaths as she came down from her climax and back to earth. Todd was standing beside the cot, smiling down at her with a satisfied expression. He grabbed a water bottle from beside the bed and took a swig. She had never felt more achingly empty in her entire life.

"You. Get. Over. Here." She rasped, pointing at Todd, then gesturing back to the bed.

"Me?" He asked, pretending to be befuddled, but the tenting of his boxers gave him away as he took a step toward her. She had him stripped down in moments.

"Sit," she commanded.

"You're bossy," he said, leaning in for a kiss. "I like it." He was teasing her, but Margery had little to no sense of humor at that exact moment. All she knew was that she needed him. *Right then.* She stood, from where she'd been lying on the bunk and making sure she wasn't going to slam her fore-head into the second bunk, she pushed Todd down to her bunk and straddled him. Before she could get totally carried away, Todd grabbed a condom from his side table and slid it on, smiling at her tenderly.

"Did you get those just for me?" Margery asked, sudden-ly fixated on the fact that Todd was, in fact, prepared for this eventuality.

"Yes."

"When?"

"Jackson Hole. Just before you got that phone call."

The phone call that had brought them back to Brewton.

"Things had been…progressing with us, and I wanted to be ready. For whenever you were."

"Todd that's so fucking sweet, I might cry." She leaned in and kissed him; once, twice. She held herself poised above him for a moment longer, and he positioned himself at her

entrance. Their eyes met, and he brushed a tender hand across her cheek. "Ready?" he asked softly.

"Ready," she said. And as she began to slide down over him, he pushed in. For a moment, there was only the warmth of his chest beneath her fingertips and the beating of their hearts, and the feeling of delicious fullness. Margery began to move, gripping Todd's shoulders for leverage to drive him harder and deeper. She wasn't sure if she was breathing as she felt him hit that perfect spot inside her that had her seeing stars.

"How..." she ground out, "how do you feel so good?"

"Right. Back. At. You, " he said between thrusts. Gone were the snarky replies from before, because Todd was lost in a realm of pleasure, too. His eyes were glassy and they almost seemed to roll back in his head as Margery set a relentless pace. His hands grasped her hips, pulling her closer and closer. Deeper and deeper. The coil in her belly tightened even more than it had when he was just using his tongue, if that were possible, and before long, they were tumbling off the edge together, each shouting the other's name like a hope for all the possibilities and probabilities during all the days to come.

They collapsed together in Margery's bunk, their limbs still intertwined, sweat from the humid night and their passionate activities coating their skin.

"That was..." Todd started.

"Yeah, it was..."Margery tried. Their eyes met where they lay, faces mere inches apart.

"Just...Wow..."Todd said, brushing the hair from her face.

"Yeah...wow," She said. "You're good at that."

"At what?" he said, a small smirk turning at the side of his mouth.

"YOU KNOW WHAT!" Margery said,glaring at him half-heartedly, with a ridiculous smile plastered to her face.

"You think so?" he asked, stroking his knuckles from her cheek bone, down her neck, and across her chest.

"Yes. Yes, I think so..."she said slowly, a wicked smile curling over her lips as the words came to her. "But, of

course, I'll have to experience a repeat performance to con-firm my findings."

"Of course," Todd said, his smile breaking open like the light of dawn. "It's only scientific."

TODD

THE NEXT DAY was filled with sorting and boxing Margery's belongings, most of which had been gratefully spared from the gasoline Shawn had splashed into the dumpster. They left a good portion of the items at her mother's house in Margery's old bedroom, but the night before, Margery had told Todd she was itching to get back on the road.

"You know, you don't have to go with me for us to be together," he'd said gently over breakfast that morning. "I can come and visit you... take nearby contracts. You could..."

"Todd," Margery said interrupting him as he tried to make his gentlemanly speech, even though the thought of her not being with him felt like absolute torture, "I still have a lot of the world to see. And you promised to show it to me."

"Well, yes, but..."

"No butts about it, Todd. I'm your passenger princess. You can't get rid of me that easily." She winked at him, and Todd felt the thrill of being teased by this woman who seemed to have blossomed right before his eyes over the past month.

"I'd never try to get rid of you," Todd said, a hand over his heart.

She smiled at him. "I know."

They ate in silence for a few moments, then Todd pulled out his phone, scrolling through messages from dispatch. "So," he said finally, "which way this time, Margery? North? South? East? West?"

He watched as her smile grew while she considered the possibilities—the probabilities; the future that she would now have...with him.

A gift, coming from what felt like a curse.

"Today seems like a nice day for going west," she said. "But can we go north again first? I'd like to see Betsy and Mike."

Todd's heart was so full of joy, it ached.

"They'd like that," he said, smiling. And leaning over the assortment of pastries on the table between them, Todd inhaled her floral scent and kissed her tenderly on the cheek.

The next day, after packing a proper bag, a few books, her comfiest jammies, and her toiletries, plus a quickly thrown together trail mix, *at Margery's request*, Todd and Margery hit the road.

"You know," he said, "this story would make a really great movie."

"Pardon?"

"You know, 'damsel in distress, kidnapped the night before her wedding, falls in love with hot trucker...'"

"Personally, I think it would make a better book," she said rummaging through her bag for her latest read, "otherwise, you know they'd cast some ugly guy who can't act as the trucker and it would all be completely ruined."

He smirked, and turned toward her.

"So you're saying I'm...not ugly?" He broadened his grin in a way he knew made his chin dimple deepen, a move which never seemed to fail him where Margery was concerned.

She let out a long-suffering sigh, but smiled at him anyway, a glimmer in her eyes.

"Just drive, Todd."

EPILOGUE
Three Months Later

MARGERY

MARGERY SAT on a bench in the shade of a flaming-red huckleberry tree, her body poised over the blank page of the notebook in her lap, clicking her pen like her life depended on it. For what felt like probably the tenth time in the last hour, she raised her hand and pen to the notebook, but no matter how she pressed the tip of her pen to the page, her mind remained a complete blank. Her face flushed in frustration, but the autumn breeze toying with the loose strands from her braid cooled her burning cheeks.

"Good boy, Barnaby!"

She heard Todd's voice before she saw him. He was wearing his customary work boots and jeans, but in the surprising warmth of the autumn day, he'd left his flannel in the truck and only wore a black cotton V-neck. He was preceded around the bend of the path that led to where she sat by a curly ball of golden fluff who barked excitedly the second he caught sight of Margery, giving the leash a hard yank as

though doing so could make the man on the other end of it walk faster. The second they were in arm's reach, Margery abandoned her notepad and pen to ruffle the fur over the puppy's ears, and as she did she felt herself inhale as her stress momentarily lessened.

"Welp. I was right. This little guy is a *genius*. It took me months to housebreak Nelson on the road, and we've only had Barnaby for what? A month?"

"I told you little Barney-Warney would get the hang of it quick. Contrary to public opinion, poodles are actually very, very smart. *Aren't they? Aren't they?*"

She was talking in that baby-doggy voice she couldn't seem to stop herself from using when Barnaby was around, and as she glanced up, she saw Todd's crooked smile as he watched her play with the dog. As though he could sense her attention shifting, Barnaby leaped up to lick her face. Then as soon as her attention was back on him, he resumed his task of staring deeply into her soul with his knowing eyes.

Barnaby, or "Barney" as they'd taken to calling him, was some sort of poodle-ish mix they'd rescued from a shelter in California at the beginning of September. They'd been there for the height of wine season, as Margery's new job as a staff writer for an up-and-coming food and travel magazine, *Eats and Beats,* along with one of the local vineyards, had been hosting a fundraiser for the small no-kill shelter. They'd been wining and dining beneath the late summer sky, Margery taking furious notes about the wine and the farm-to-table dishes being presented at the event, when volunteers began walking around the venue with various adoptable dogs. It only took one look into his hazel eyes, and Barnaby had snatched both of their hearts straight out of their chests. They'd filled out all of the paperwork to bring him home that very day.

"I know adopting a dog wasn't exactly *why* we were at that event, but it was certainly a happy accident," Margery commented to Todd later that night as they lay in their bunks, Barney snoring softly in his new doggy bed by Margery's feet.

"Just one of the many happy probabilities I've stumbled upon by accident lately," Todd mused, chuckling. In the dark, his laughter rolled over her skin like a caress.

The writing job was another happy probability she supposed, as she lay in the dark that night thinking about all the steps that led her to this moment, right there and then. She'd submitted a freelance article to *Eats and Beats* in mid-July after their second visit to Betsy and Mike's, proclaiming to Todd, "The world needs to know about this place!"

The editor had written back less than a week later saying, "I'm not sure I've ever read an article that made me hungrier," and practically begged her to consider their vacant staff writer position.

"They don't want anyone else to scoop you up!" Todd had said to her, beaming as she'd read him the email, his eyes straying from the road to look at her. "And I can't say that I blame them," he'd winked.

She'd taken the job, not knowing if she could recreate the magic of that first article, or not, but wanting desperately to try.

And somehow she had, she'd written a half dozen articles in the past two months alone, as Todd kept taking the contract routes that led him to his favorite hole-in-the-wall places. And though Margery had hardly set a foot outside Brewton, Alabama until a couple of months earlier, she was finding life on the road suited her. Eating delicious food all day every day suited her. Writing also suited her. Life with Todd suited her, too.

Which was why it was so frustrating that her current article seemed to be giving her so much trouble.

"Struggling?" Todd asked, seeing her lost in her storm of thoughts. He sat down beside her on the bench, holding Barney by the collar to keep him from leaping at the tires of a passing bicyclist.

"Yeah," she said, "I can't figure out why this one is so much harder to write."

"Do you think it could be because this one's personal?"

he asked softly, tracing the back of her hand with the rough pad of his thumb.

"Yeah...maybe," she said. She leaned her head on Todd's shoulder and inhaled his scent; musky and spicy with just a hint of that smell that she'd begun to identify as "being on the road".

"Take a walk with me," Todd said, almost abruptly. "Rumor has it, there's a gorgeous waterfall just over there." He stood and winked at her, cajoling her to take a break from her writing and come along, but she saw the deep affection and tenderness hiding behind his laughing eyes.

Stuffing her notebook and pen into her crossbody bag, she slung it behind her back and grabbed his hand.

"That sounds like just what I need."

THEY STROLLED down the path, Barnaby in tow, until the roar of the waterfall was almost too loud to make easy conversation. When they descended the steps to the observation platform, Margery's jaw dropped. There before her, was the most beautiful volcanically formed waterfall she'd ever seen. *Not that I've even seen a volcanically formed waterfall before, but...whatever.*

Still, this one seemed special. The water moved in a joyful torrent, throwing itself over the sharp black edge of the volcanic stone and splattering the lichen-covered canyon walls, shimmering with rainbows in the autumn sunlight. The billboard at the beginning of the trail had told of the destruction by the last major volcanic event in the Yellowstone caldera, and of how, over the millennia, the quiet certitude of the Snake River had slowly, but surely, worn away the stone enough to form this incredible waterfall.

What looked like destruction, made space for the most beautiful creation.

And there she had it—the angle for her story.

L ATER THAT NIGHT, with the road rumbling away beneath them in the cab of the truck, and her computer resting on her lap, Margery wrote:

"If you had stood on the edge of all that fire and ash all those millennia ago, they would have called it destruction. Thankfully, neither Nature, nor God concern themselves with our human timetables or limited understandings of their creative endeavors, and neither does time. Instead, they wait patiently for the lava to cool, then slowly erode beneath the waters of the Snake River. They wait for the carving of the black canyon walls, for the growth of the lichens, and for the staggering beauty of a rainbow waterfall.

Then, astonishingly, they watch us humans come and admire their feat for a whole five minutes before going back to the stagnant lives those humans were already living, and will continue to live if not for a dramatic twist of fate.

The reality is that few are willing to risk the kind of creativity that first requires a level of destruction. Be it leaving a soul sucking job, an abusive relationship, or a harmful system, most of us will choose the devil we know over the fear of the great unknown.

Yes, I blew up my life when I left my ex-fiancée the night before our wedding. I left behind my job, my expected place in society, and the friends who thought they knew me. But the most important person I met when I left it all behind wasn't actually the handsome trucker with whom I am now deeply in love.

It was myself.

So if you too find yourself standing at a crossroads in your life, pondering: Should I stay? Or should I go?—

If you find yourself contemplating the possibilities of leaving something old behind, in hopes of embarking on a new adventure—

I hope you'll take the leap over the edge of that lava

stone cliff with me, and let the light hit you in all your brilliance. Let the fire take all that cannot withstand it. Dare to make space for something new."

TODD

TODD LOOKED up at Margery with tears in his eyes, his heart filllled to the brim with an unfamiliar tightening. She turned towards him with her steaming mug of tea cupped in her hands, and upon seeing his expression, she nearly dropped it.

"Oh my God. Is the article that bad?" she asked, her eyes widening, cheeks flushing in that adorable way they always did when she felt any kind of strong emotion.

"No! No, baby...it's..." He trailed off. It was impossible to find adequate words to express how beautiful her article had been, but the worried look on her face compelled him to try."It's beautiful," he said, setting down the pages on the console between them and reaching across to touch her forearm.

"You really think so?"

"I know so. They're going to love it. And if they don't, send it somewhere else."

"Okay," she said, smiling. She set her mug down between them and reached over to wipe the tear away from his stubbled cheek. "You know, I'm not sure I've ever made a grown man cry before."

"Well, keep writing like this and you're going to see it at least once a week."

"Maybe someday I'll tell the whole story."

"Maybe," he said, smiling gently, "when you're ready."

Just then Barney woke up from his puppy nap and leaped onto the console, knocking over the typed draft of the article, and nearly upsetting Margery's mug of steaming tea. Thankfully, Todd's trucker reflexes kicked in, and though he could not prevent the puppy prints that landed on the pages,

he was able to save both the mug from breaking and the tea from spilling.

"And THIS, Margery my dear, is why you should use paper to-go cups, not irreplaceable hand-thrown mugs you can only get in Black Forest Colorado." He gave her his signature crooked smile and winked.

"Todd, DARLING, you know I'm saving the planet, one less to-go cup at a time. Your granola eating, tree hugging ass ought to appreciate that." She reclaimed her mug from Todd's grasp and lifted it to her lips. Barney had plopped his curly golden head in her lap, and she raised her free hand to give him his customary morning scratches behind the ears.

"Have I mentioned you're getting feistier by the minute?" he said as he put the key in the ignition, starting the truck for their long drive for the day. They were picking up a load bound for Utah next.

"And you love me for it," she said, looking at him with none of the teasing her words implied; her eyes only that crystalline blue, the sweet smell of strawberries wafting from her freshly washed hair, no shadow of death hanging over her. Instead, she projected only hope and possibility.

How it was always meant to be.

"Yes," he said, his warm eyes meeting hers. "Yes, I do."

ACKNOWLEDGMENTS

I want to thank my husband Willy Kelley; my best road trip buddy, and fellow good-food-enthusiast. The roadtrip adventures we have experienced together over the past fifteen years made good inspiration for this story and—even though, like Todd, you insist on taking unflattering sleeping pictures of me while we drive—I hope you know that adventuring with you is my very favorite thing.

Thank you to my Spicy Dragon Ladies Book Club, for enthusiastically reading the earlier drafts of this story; and to Sadie specifically, my 'queen of smut', thank you for encouraging me that my sex scene was cute and not cringe.

Thank you to my editor Linda Slate, who took what I thought was a grammatically correct manuscript, and actually made it into one. I am so incredibly grateful for your expertise and help, and please consider yourself hired for the next book!

Thank you to my wonderful cover designer My Lan Khuc, who brought the vision and the vibes of the cover to life with her incredible talent and skill. I can't wait for our next project together!

Thank you to my brother L.A. Morton-Yates, my co-conspirator at Synthesis Press; your help with all the administrative tasks it takes to publish a book is appreciated as always. Your book next? ;)

Thank you to all my early readers of *Just Drive* when it was being written serially on Substack; your weekly encouragement helped me write this novella in record time, and your comments helped me keep the story on track. I hope you find this more polished and complete version even more delightful to read than the first.

And to you, my dear readers; thank you for joining me on this adventure. *Just Drive* is not only a love story between Todd and Margery, but it is a also a sort of love note dedicated to roadtrips, good food, and to the unique places that have the capacity to change us for the better. Getting to write this was so much fun, and having you share the adventure by reading it, is even better.

Now, go tell all your friends.

ABOUT THE AUTHOR

Grace E. Kelley is a poet, personal essayist, and speculative storyteller. Across the varied genres she explores, she writes with the intent to help her readers name what aches in their own experience, so that they can move towards greater wholeness and freedom. *Just Drive* is her first fiction publication, but it is certainly not her last.

Be sure to subscribe to her newsletter, *Tell Me a Story* (synthesisstories.substack.com) to keep up to date on all her latest fiction projects. And check out synthesispress.com to see her other titles.

A Shade. A Storm. A Soul.

Cursed with forbidden knowledge, 19-year-old Dela must hide her secret from her nomadic tribe or face exile into the frozen wasteland of the Bitters. When she becomes separated from her people during a blizzard, a mysterious and dangerous Synderer named Talon promises to help her find her way back to them. She quickly learns that nothing is what it seems, that her curse may actually be a gift, and that the Bitters are far more dangerous than she could have imagined.

Packed with unexpected twists, Bittersouls is a mixture of survival, adventure, and slow-burn romance that is sure to get your heart pounding.

PROLOGUE

THE FIRST TIME Dela saw the Jackal, it didn't try to kill her. It was a chilly night, but the little girl didn't notice. She was young, still so full of Warmth. The wind blew snow flurries around the camp, shimmering like stars in the firelight. She giggled as she kicked a smooth stone from snowbank to snowbank. The older snow had melted and frozen on the surface just thick enough for the stone to bounce instead of sink.

Her laughter was accompanied by the sounds of merriment behind her. The adults of the congregation were still hard at work on the fifth evening of the Festival of Three Flames, and Dela was long supposed to be tucked away with the other children in their beds. They couldn't hear her over the noise of their lively conversations, pumping bellows, and roaring flames. She didn't spare them much thought; they wouldn't even notice she was gone. She could watch as long as she wanted, then slink back to bed. No one would be the wiser.

She wasn't sure why she was awake. The other children didn't wonder about it, apparently. A feast involving weeks of arduous labor, held once every five years in this very spot. How could she not be curious? After all, she was practically grown up at almost five years old. It was right for her to wonder what this occasion involved, and why her parents and the others were so adamant about its importance.

But she hadn't wondered about it for long. She'd found the stone, then chased it as it skipped and slid through the snow-washed darkness. The fire was only fifty feet behind her, but in her mind it was already a world away.

Dela snickered as she kicked the stone again, pointing as if it had told a joke when it skidded to a stop. She skipped toward it, beaming as brightly as the moon high above the

concealing clouds. The stone was glossy in her hand, shaved smooth by time and ice. She stared into it, her grin bubbling over into another giggle.

A warm wall of whiteness rose above her, blocking the wind and snow.

Dela looked up slowly, marveling at the creature's angular grace. It dipped its head, sniffing at her midnight hair. She gasped at the smell of its breath, like smoke and rosehips. It examined her with keen eyes, tilting its head slightly.

"Pu…" The word was lost in her wonder. "Puppy?"

She raised a hand to touch its snout, but it leaped away. Its limbs were sharp as bones, its ears pointed as knife blades. She'd heard rhymes about the creatures they called Jackals but had never seen one herself. It was beautiful.

She didn't wait for it to go. The adults would want to see it. It was so pretty. So regal. They had to know it was here to visit them. Maybe they would want to pet it.

She ran for the firelight, the rock she'd been chasing long forgotten. She hollered and laughed, plunging past the tent line and into the writhing mass of the congregation. The cold of the night fell away like a discarded cloak, replaced by the dry heat of the furnace at the center of it all. Some eyes followed her, but most were still too busy with their work. The bellows wouldn't pump themselves. Even for the interruption of a child long thought to be abed, the work could not be stopped.

A hand caught her arm, and the little girl whirled to find her father frowning down at her. "Adelaide," he growled, crouching to her level.

"Papa." Her smile widened. "Puppy!"

She pointed past the people and their festival, out into the dark and the cold of the night.

"What are you talking about, Adelaide?" her father asked, the quiet sharpness of a deep-seated worry taking shape in his voice.

"It's pretty, Papa." She jumped up and down, trying to get him to look where she was pointing. What if it moved? What if it left before he followed her? She lowered her voice, as if conferring an important secret to the man. "It's a Jackal."

"Oh, Rolf." Her mother appeared as if out of nowhere, putting a hand on the man's shoulder. "You know she's just making up stories, trying to find a reason to join us out here." She crouched beside the little girl, who pouted back at her.

"Isn't that right, Adelaide? All the light and the noise and the excitement?"

"No, it's—"

"It's okay, Adelaide. I'm not angry." She smiled, warm and genuine. The girl almost folded at that. She loved her mother, and she knew the woman loved her, too. "Don't you think we should go back to bed?"

"But the Jackal," Dela whimpered. "It's so pretty. And nice!"

"That's nice, Adelaide." The woman picked her up, carrying her gently back toward the tent. "I'm sure it will still be there in the morning. Maybe we can meet it then."

"No, Mama!" The little girl fought against her mother's hold. Didn't they believe her? They had to believe her. "He's nice! He's come to be my friend."

"That's good, little cub." The woman stooped through the thick leathery flap of the tent, fastening it behind her. She set the girl down on the deep plush of her fur sleeping mat, wrapping her carefully in the extremities of the pelt.

"Don't you want to meet my friend?" the little girl pleaded.

Her mother's caring expression slowly grew stern as she studied the girl's face. Now she believed her, Dela could tell. So why wasn't she excited, too?

"How about a story, little cub?"

Dela didn't give up her pout, but nodded meekly. "What about?"

"Well…" Her mother tapped her chin. "You wanted to know about the festival, didn't you? How about a story about that?"

The little girl considered for a moment, then nodded again. "Okay."

"All right. Get comfortable, little cub."

She did so, wiggling and squirming until she'd found just the right position for sleeping. "Ready, Mama."

"Hmm. Have you heard anything about the Three Flames?"

Dela shook her head. "Not a lot, Mama."

"Well, long ago, the world was a beautiful, warm place. People lived together in camps that never moved, hundreds upon hundreds of them. The herds were always plentiful, and snow only covered the ground a small portion of the year."

"When, Mama?" The girl shook her head. "Was it like that when you were my age?"

The woman laughed. "No, little cub. This was a long time before that. A dozen Warmthtimes at least before I was born. There's been… I don't even know if they count anymore. Thirty Festivals since then?"

The little girl nodded.

"In those days, there was only One Flame that burned high and bright in the sky, uncovered by clouds and snowfall. People should have been happy, but they were not grateful for what they had. The great deceiver, Bale the Omnivolent, promised them they could have more. That if they followed his instructions, they could have not One Flame, but Three.

"The people of the world were foolish. They took his offer, not questioning what it meant. No light or life comes from nothing. Bale split the One Flame, giving to each man, woman, and child a Flame Within."

"But Mama," Dela said. "Isn't that where our Warmth comes from?"

"Of course, little cub." Her mother nodded. "Such a smart

girl. But you have to remember, the world wasn't frozen in those days. We didn't need Warmth to live. But now, with the One Flame spread like ashes in the wind, every one of us must clutch at every bit of Warmth we can hold on to. That's why we need the Congregation."

The little girl nodded. "'We share our Warmth, so none may go cold.'"

The woman's smile widened. "You've been paying attention to your lessons, haven't you?"

Dela giggled, nodding.

"Well, that's good. Do you know what happened to the rest of what Bale stole from the One Flame?"

The little girl shook her head.

"He seeded the ground with the black salt of the Flame Without. Not everywhere, though. Only a few places have the salt, like the one we're camped around right now."

"But what's it for, Mama?"

"You know the blacksticks that all the grown-ups have?"

"The ones that help them start fires?"

Her mother nodded. "That's the third Flame. The Flame Without. This whole festival is our way of showing penitence for the mistakes of our ancestors. And by the mercy of the One, we can make the blacksticks here as part of our worship."

The little girl nodded slowly, then frowned. "But Mama, you said there were hund… hundre… lots of people. What happened to them?"

"That's why I'm telling you this story, little cub." The woman sighed, eyes falling to her lap. "The deceiver gave one more thing to some alongside the Flame Within. The Ministers have it mentioned in their texts as the Shadow, but most people just call it madness. When the Bitter Wind came and nature itself was changed, the people and creatures of the world grew frightful. Twisted. Corrupt. Not everyone found safe ways to live like we did."

"Mama?" Dela pursed her lips. "This doesn't seem like a very good story."

"It's not," her mother admitted. "But like most stories, it's told for a reason."

"What's that, Mama?"

The woman leaned close to her daughter, whispering carefully into the little girl's ear, "You need to understand that Jackals aren't animals. They aren't something you can turn into a pet, nor even something truly wild. They are his, Adelaide. Do you understand? They are mad, and they bring madness. If you ever see one, you must tell no one."
Dela shivered. She understood completely, so far as a little girl could.

"And if you see anything after," her mother added, "that is a secret you must keep until the day your Warmth runs out."

**KEEP READING DELA'S ADVENTURE
AND GET YOUR GET YOUR COPY
OF BITTERSOULS TODAY!**

9 798986 602295